Aftermath of the Dead

Aftermath of the Dead

Gregory Smith

iUniverse, Inc.
New York Lincoln Shanghai

Aftermath of the Dead

Copyright © 2005 by Gregory Smith

All rights reserved. No part of this book may be used or reproduced by any means, graphic, electronic, or mechanical, including photocopying, recording, taping or by any information storage retrieval system without the written permission of the publisher except in the case of brief quotations embodied in critical articles and reviews.

iUniverse books may be ordered through booksellers or by contacting:

iUniverse
2021 Pine Lake Road, Suite 100
Lincoln, NE 68512
www.iuniverse.com
1-800-Authors (1-800-288-4677)

ISBN-13: 978-0-595-35934-9 (pbk)
ISBN-13: 978-0-595-80388-0 (ebk)
ISBN-10: 0-595-35934-5 (pbk)
ISBN-10: 0-595-80388-1 (ebk)

Printed in the United States of America

ACKNOWLEDGMENTS

I wish to thank a very important person, in my knowledge and storytelling of the 'fantastique' who unfortunately is no longer with us, Aristide Massaccesi aka Joe D'Amato. Thank you so much my friend. *Riposarsi nella pace il mio amico.*

Also I wish to thank 'A', You never knew how much you influenced and meant to me, but I'm glad you were in my life.

1

Introduction

Location: **Saint Louis Missouri USA**
Date: **October 28, 2006**

Everything in life is changing in St. Louis. Summer time is fading; each of the days gets a little shorter with each sunset that disappears in the western sky. The temperature as well is changing into it's annual pattern of much cooler days with even crisper nights. The residents of St. Louis are changing as well. They're gearing up for the annual snow fall and the inevitable challenges of the approaching winter storms. Every day is now cherished as last chances because when the approaching winter comes, outside activity grinds to a stand still. This results in more time being spent inside of the house but for now it's beautiful. The roasting oven feel of the summer heat trapped in the concrete has left.

All that remains now are gorgeous sixty five degree autumn days. The leaves on the trees are in their full fall foliage. Brilliant shades of golden browns are intermixed with spectacular reds which dangle helplessly from the branches high above. Then litter the ground below as they fall. Everyone is very excited to be through the summer heat, but also feel a sense dread as they know old man winter will arrive shortly.

But, for now atleast everyone is going through his or her daily routine just like any other fall morning. Commuters are hitting the highway making their daily journey to work in the city from the outlying suburbs. School children board their school bus to head off to their classes, but inside the children's minds their imaginations are already well into the thoughts of Halloween and trick-or-treating for delicious candy. Yet, unknown to the residents of St. Louis and beyond the city limit's are the actions going on deep inside the research facilities of the major area hospitals located in the city. These activities will change their lives forever. As, well as humanities.

Since the terrorist attacks on 9-11 and then the subsequent formation of The Department of Homeland Security Office, a section of the law was to allow the following. All local hospitals to be linked via a Local Area Network (LAN), which has allowed them to combine all of their research and development activities. The purpose of the Bush Administration proposal, was to prevent a biological outbreak of smallpox and other airborne agents from terrorist attacks spreading out of control. The main benefit the hospitals have seen is that this legislation will help them save cost where their research efforts overlap. One just has to love our capitalist system!

Contributing extensively to the project are two of the biggest and most respected hospitals in the country. They are St. Louis University (SLU) located in South City off from Grand Boulevard and the second being Barnes Jewish Hospital (BJC) located in the Central West End neighborhood off from Lindell Avenue. Together, they are the two major hospitals that are linked via the LAN. Their research effort, at the moment is in the genetic cell regeneration field. By manipulating the way the individual cells respond to one another, scientist have in essence caused the cells to function longer than they were designed to. The result is increased time the skin maintains a more youthful appearance, as well as for a longer duration. Because of the now combined research effort, the time to develop this new wonder drug as been cut from approximately ten to just over four years. The purpose of the tests and trials is to find an anti-aging drug that can be marketed to consumers who feel you

Introduction 3

are eighty but should look thirty. The potential sales to the consumer segment, could be in the billions for the drug and cosmetics companies. All for vanity of our western society. As, well in our never ending quest to elude death, huh?

The clinical trails are set to begin on October 29, 2006 at St. Louis University Hospital. Right now the main chemicals, involved are being transported as we speak. The chemical compound is being supplied by a major bioengineering company located in St. Louis, which manufactures everything from bio engineered seeds to lawn and garden herbicides. Entrusted with this cargo is a specialized medical delivery company, called Express Delivery.

2

Outbreak

TIME: 11:29 A.M. CENTRAL STANDARD TIME

Heading east on Highway 44 Michael Whitman, a courier for Express Delivery. The company is located in Saint Charles, Missouri. The city of St. Charles is a suburb of St. Louis City filled with those that fled the hassles of city life and prefer a overcrowded and overpriced life. Express Delivery specializes in the medical test delivery business. Michael is on his route hauling the usual assortments of blood tests, urine tests, and other lab specimens.

He takes his standard route to St. Louis University (SLU) and will exit at Grand Boulevard, still two miles ahead. Traffic is quite light at this time of day. Most from the morning gridlock has passed and the evening ride home is still well over five hours away. Suddenly out the corner of his left eye, he notices in his side mirror two cars approaching quickly. Michael intentionally slows his Ford Econline van down enough to piss off this jerk who is tailgating him. Checking his mirror again, Michael catches a Mustang trying to sneak in front of him attempting to make it's exit onto Kingshighway Boulevard.

Without warning, the car slams into his rear end. With the van's high profile and the combined speed the two vehicles are traveling, the velocity of the impact is so great that it sends Michael's van rolling violently on it's right side. The damage to the van is immediate and disastrous for Michael. The Mustang meanwhile begins fishtailing and smacks hard against the concrete barrier. With dust and debris flying high into the air, the van flips over one final time before stopping on it's side halfway down the Kingshighway exit ramp. Immediately, other travelers from the highway depart from their cars to try and help-out the destroyed van. Some tend to the wrecked Mustang, as well. Within seconds over ten drivers have stopped and are doing as much, as they can to assist the injured drivers.

Michael is trapped upside down and slumped unconscious in his shattered van. He is bleeding heavily and lies mangled in the twisted confines of metal and crushed glass. At the scene of the second accident, the four occupants from the car emerge staggering from the wrecked American sports car with minor superficial cuts to their faces. The two guys are wearing trucker style caps on their heads. They're holding their foreheads which are lightly bleeding as they desperately try to grab hold of their young girlfriends. The girls are crying and are stunned from the hard impact. All of this due to the carelessness of the testosterone filled, impatient driver.

At 911 emergency dispatch, the operator on duty is inundated with frantic calls from horrified motorists at the crash scene. Less than four minutes later, three ambulances and two police vehicles arrive on the scene. Immediately, the officers try to gain control over and redirect the curious onlookers. The police goal is to clear the scene for the paramedics, so they can tend to the injured and save lives, like they do all day, every day. Routinely, like thousands of calls prior the paramedics attend to Michael's wounds; as the blood pressure cuff is attached they immediately detect that the victim is non responsive and does not have a pulse. A male paramedic runs to Michael's aid with a C-spine. Without hesitation, he slides it through the driver's side door that was torn off by the jaws of life, just moments ago. A second paramedic is waiting inside the van hovering above Michael. The paramedic in the interior grabs it from his colleague and moves it into position wedging it smoothly in between Michael's lifeless body and the van's interior.

"He's critical and unresponsive!" A paramedic shouts.

The medic quickly tapes Michael's forehead down tightly to the C-spine. No movement from his neck is tolerated. This preventive measure is to ensure there is no further injury to his neck or spine which may occur during the extraction process. Three medics, are waiting outside the van, they receive the top of the C-spine and carefully begin to extract Michael out from his crushed metal tomb. He shows, no signs of life when he is removed from the van. Immediately, the paramedics begin to try to bring Michael back from death.

Free from the restraints of the van, the two paramedics can finally begin CPR on him. One, two, three they inflate Michael's lungs with air. Nothing…one, two, three and again his lungs are filled with oxygen. Still his vitals are flat. With the golden hour slipping through the precious hour glass. They open their box filled with supplies and prep him for the defibrillator.

The paramedics apply the sticky pads to his body. They are placed over his heart and the right side of his chest simultaneously, the defibrillator is charged and ready for use.

"Clear!"

The medics all move away from their patient. The paddles hit his chest and discharge electricity, his lifeless body heaves from the jolt of powerful electricity. Following the first shock of electricity the paramedic, checks his vital signs again. Still, his vitals show nothing.

At the rear of the delivery van, the cargo doors pop-open. Inside, something breaks free from the nylon straps that was holding it in place. A large crushing sound as it begins passing over top of the various medical tests, which were due to be delivered. What is it? A large barrel containing a thick powder substance. The constancy is like liquid. It comes rolling out and with each second, the barrel builds even greater momentum. It comes flying out of the van smacking the ground with a thud. The object must weigh at least a hundred pounds. The barrel rolls quickly down the slopped exit ramp opposite of the way traffic normal flows. Finally, it stops, as it hit's the Fire and Rescue truck. It's former occupants are assisting their critically injured patent. The stainless steel front bumper of the truck stops the massive barrel in a instant. The lid pops open and a small amount of powder begins to spill out. It continues to spill along the roadside without anyone noticing.

In the background of all this chaotic happening's is the sound of the medics shocking Michael's body a second then a third and a dastardly fourth and final time. Finally, the frantic occupants from the car emerge from a state of shock to witness the medics abandoning their efforts on trying to retrieve Michael from his current state.

Michael Fitch is pronounced dead at 11:36 am. The young teenage girl from the Mustang begins crying and yelling at the driver who, he himself can not be more than twenty years old. A police office pulls the teen aside and the medics pass by her with Michael on the stretcher on their way towards the ambulance. Then two feet before being loaded in the back of the ambulance. Michael's torso twitches for a split second. No one notices this action or maybe they do but justify this, in their minds as a result of the energy still stored up within his nerves and muscles. Another second passes, he twitches a second time. This time even more so. Then unexpectedly, Michael sits up.

A male medic nearest to him yells to his partner.

"Jerry, Get over here, now!" Then to Michael, "Sir, are you okay?"

Michael gives no audible response, just a blank expression which is painted on his face. His eyes do not focus on anything and his gaze is miles away. His facial expression is awkward and he doesn't seem to know where in the world, he is. He could be in either St. Louis or St. Paul, he wouldn't know the difference. Again the paramedic tries to communicate with Michael to see if he is all right. Still silence. Then a female medic approaches him to take his vitals. She wraps the blood pressure cuff around his biceps and affixes the Velcro straps to tighten it around his upper arm. As, the medic begins to pump the ball to tighten the cuff to obtain the results, Michael begins to wail in discomfort.

The paramedic attempts to calm Michael down by telling him that everything is all right and soon he'll be on his way to the emergency room at St. Louis University Hospital. Michael jerks violently away, quickly breaking free from the medic's grasp. The female medic loses her balance, stumbles and falls against the stretcher. As, the paramedic tries to gain her bearings, Michael sits up from the stretcher quickly grabs the paramedic's left arm.

"Let my arm go, now!"

She yells to him. Michael looks puzzled at the woman and in one swift motion he lowers his head and sinks his teeth deep into her forearm. The medic immediately begins to scream from the painful bite. The medic manages to jerk away from his grasp.

"John, for God's sake help me get this guy off, this jerk just bit me!"

Michael moves towards her but falls from the stretcher down to the pavement. Two male medics run over to help their partner. One paramedic tends to the injured woman, while the other tries to restrain Michael. He grabs the enraged man underneath his armpit and attempts to hoist the uncommunicative man up. Still, Michael continues to fight with the medic by kicking and swinging his arms wildly about.

Suddenly, Michael gets loose and falls back to the ground, on his back. Abruptly, he jumps to his feet and lunges at the medic. In a instant Michael rips into the man's neck. The injured medic screams for his life. A police officer hears the screams and pleas for assistance. The officer shifts his attention from the girl involved in the second car and runs around the front hood of the ambulance. As, he rounds the hood he finds Michael on top of the male medic tearing into his throat with his hungry mouth. He is yanking flesh out with his sharp teeth. Blood pours out of the medics body and begins saturating the ground as, well as staining the grass and weeds that grow without worry along side the road. The startled cop orders the man to get up and to place his hands behind his back. The officer gets no response from Michael.

The police officer approaches Michael with caution. He draws his sidearm and points it at the unresponsive man. Without warning Michael leaps at the officer and charges toward him. The young officer is only in his second year on the force and reacts with haste. He fires three shots at Michael. The bullets thunderously penetrate his chest and knock him back. After stumbling backwards a couple of steps from the impact, Michael continues towards the scared officer. The facial expression of the officer tells it all. He is in total shock and denial, yet still manages to fire off two more shots. The first one misses completely, the second hit's Michael in the thigh, but it doesn't slow him down in the least.

The officer decides that he needs to change his tactics. Obviously, his current actions are not are working like, he would have wished for. He quickly runs behind the rear of the ambulance and takes cover. Panicked, he looks over and sees the female medic wondering aimlessly. He yells to her.

"Get on the radio and get some back-up out here!"

When the officer receives no response from the medic, he yells even louder this time.

"What the fuck are you waiting for? This jerk killed your partner! Hurry!"

She turns to face him and stares at him with that same blank look that he just saw on Michael. The officer yells over to her again.

"What are you waiting for? Fuckin' do it, now!"

At that instant, Michael comes stumbling around the front end of the ambulance. He's dragging his right leg which is cocked at a ninety degree angle, to the side. It drags along the roadside, but it doesn't seem to hamper his mobility or even slow him down. Michael doesn't even hold his injured appendage. Or even favor it in the least. How can he possibly tolerate the amount of pain, that he must be experiencing, right now?

It's possible the officer would love to know the answer to that question. Along with how, he's walking after the three shots to his chest? The wounds aren't even bleeding. The damaged flesh from the impact is all that you can see. The officer just looks in awe at the sight in front of his eyes. He turns to yell once again at the female medic, but this time she's suddenly out of his sight. He thinks to himself.

"Wow if she's smart, she got the hell out of here."

On top of the ambulance there's a loud metallic crunching noise. The roof of the ambulance crumbles under the stress of the compact weight of the object. The police officer looks up and to his amazement. It's the female medic. She leaps from the ambulance landing on top of the officer. The bewildered officer frantically struggles against the woman. He can't manage to shake her off. During the struggle, the medic manages to clamp down on the police officer's forearm.

"AWAH!!"

Immediately, the officer screams in torment but somehow manages to get a handle on the medics arm. He throws her with all of his might against the side of the ambulance. The officer struggles to get back to his feet, overwhelmed with pain from the vicious wound. The moment the crowd of onlookers spot the cop's injuries, they begin to panic and scream. One of the onlookers is a long haul truck driver, who is carrying a full load of frozen chicken. Moments prior, the truck driver jumped down from his eighteen-wheeler to help the police officer and runs right into Michael.

Michael charges at the fleeing truck driver and grabs hold of him. His teeth clamp down on the first thing, he can grasp his forearm. The driver desperately tries to escape from Michael, as blood begins to gush out of his wound. Witnessing even more destruction the crowd scatters, fleeing in any direction that is away from Michael and his victims. One of the fleeing bystanders is the teen girl from the Mustang. She freaks out from the traumatic situation running directly into the lanes of flowing eastbound traffic. The frighten girl narrowly misses one SUV by less than a foot. As, she enters the third east bound lane, WHAM! She is slammed into by a speeding Dodge pickup truck.

The truck and it's driver have no time to stop and the five thousand pound vehicle slams into her body with full punishing force. Several other of the cars that are traveling behind the truck, set off a chain reaction as more cars, trucks and suv's have no room to move and shatter into the back of each other. Brakes lock up, tires smoke followed by the horrendous sound of metal colliding with metal. When it's all said and done, ten cars are pilled up on top of each other. Thick chocking clouds of black smoke billow in the air from the stalled-out engine bays. The people who stopped for the original accident do not attempt to help these new accident victims; instead all they want to do is to escape the horror before them on the Kingshighway exit ramp.

Some of the spectators try to return to their cars, but Michael and the newly reanimated female medic turn their attention away from the cop and the truck driver to stop them. Instead, the two focus their attention on as many possible victims left on the highway as possible to attack. Their focus narrows to, two women in their mid forties. The women attempt to get inside of their cars, believing they'll be safe from the strange happening's occurring on Highway 44. Michael catch's up to the woman running for the drivers seat and knocks her down to the ground. She's screaming pleading for her life yet still that blank look on Michael's face remains still and unemotional. Thus her pleas for mercy from her attacker do nothing to help her plight. Michael rips into her pudgy flesh like boiling water over a full pot of spaghetti noodles.

The ladies companion is fairing little better as the female medic begins to chase her down the exit ramp of Highway 44 and finally onto Kingshighway Boulevard. Unfortunately, the fleeing woman trips on the steeply graded grass and falls head first. She, begins to roll down the hill violently. Luckily, for her the insane medic slips down on her backside as well and she too slides the entire way down the embankment. The startled woman from the highway is on her knees trying to regain her composure when she notices the medic is still approaching her. The medic is stumbling on rubbery legs as it approaches the woman. The lady has the good sense to get up and atleast attempt to flee. The medic chases the woman onto Kingshighway and they both head north on the very busy road.

The terrorized woman manages to avoid the approaching traffic that is moving south. Not a single person at all will stop for her; the only reaction she receives from the drivers are for them to speed up and honk their horns at her. The terrified woman attempts to gain attention to her plight by waving her arms up and down in a desperate attempt to get someone to stop. Several more cars sail past her and speed up. Finally, a St. Louis City Road Department truck stops on the gravel shoulder of Kingshighway and before the truck stops, the woman comes running up quickly to the truck's door. A black heavyset man opens the heavy metal orange door.

The woman's already up on the running board as the door is opened. The surprised man attempts to find from her what is going on. But, she's yelling at the driver incoherently.

"I need to know what's goin' on if you want my help. Do you understand anything 'am sayin to you?"

Quickly, she turns around before answering the man and sees that the whacked out female medic is just one hundred yards away from her. But, situated in the background are three more blank empty faced creatures, as they stumble their way down the exit ramp. For a second time, the woman pleads for the men in the truck. She pleads for them to get out from the truck and stop that woman. The truck driver and his fellow workers look at the woman confused at her demands. Again, the driver yells at the woman.

"Did that woman hit you?"

Desperately, she pleads again for his help to stop the approaching woman and now the other three that have followed it onto Kingshighway in pursuit of her. Then in a given up tone, she says to the truck driver.

"They're dead. They're already dead. They've killed my sister."

3

11:42 A.M. October 28, 2006

The statement by the woman is finally enough to grab hold of the road crew's attention. In unison all four men depart from the cab of the truck. A burly white guy is carrying a long 18-inch steel pipe and his buddy, a slim tall black guy is handling a large heavy wrench. The female medic stops in the median of the road and within moments the other three creatures come together. The group appears to be formulating a plan together, though they don't speak to each other. The truck driver yells at them.

"Hey! Whatda fuck you guys doin'?"

He receives no response back from the four creatures standing in the middle of Kingshighway. This is the type of guy most of us would never want to piss off. But, these four don't really seem worried about the four truckers approaching them with weapons in tow. On cue the four awkward moving creatures begin to move with a sole purpose in the direction of the four approaching city workers.

On the east bound Highway 44. Michael is heaving over the Romanesque woman. The blood from her several neck wounds has spilled itself all over the breakdown lane in those deep machined channels. Michael's eyes are empty, as people continue to flee. But, amongst all the destruction a door opens among the twisted metal that has shut down the east bound lane Highway 44. As sudden as a shark's attack, Michael jumps back to it's feet and is hovering over his victim like a lion would over his kill. The door cracks open even further, the suv is piled up ten feet in the air situated on top of a truck and a sports car. Inside the vehicle, a teenage girl with blonde hair looks out and sees Michael and the male medic down below. The girl is injured, bleeding profusely from her forehead. She screams out in a whinny voice.

"Hey, help me! You two help!"

The two creatures start stumbling towards the helpless naive girl, she looks over and sees the male medic. Then she begins to freak out.

"What the fuck is wrong with you? Don't come up here, I mean it!"

The two on the ground don't say anything, yet they continue walking towards her. She starts to panic and shakes her companion who is slumped over on the driver's door.

"Hey, Tim! Wake up! You have to. Wake up now!"

Tim doesn't wake up on her demand. "You jerk." She tries again "You gotta wake up. There are these freaks coming."

Michael and the male medic are down at the base of the accident. The hungry creatures try and climb up to the mound of cars but fail and fall back to the ground, which is now coated with slick engine oil. Again and again the creatures repeatedly try in vain to climb up to the hopeless girl.

The terrified girl reaches down in-between her bucket seat and unlatches her safety belt. Immediately, she falls forward landing on the cracked dashboard. Quickly, she climbs over her seat and enters in the rear bench. Narrow droplets of blood follow her. Outside the suv Michael and the medic don't seem to know what to do. The two creatures stay in the same spot trying to climb-up to a prey that is no longer there. Then there's movement again in the cab but outside Michael and the medic are still trying to climb the heap of metal. She looks back and sees Tim moving around in his seat.

"Help me, Tim!"

She screams. Her boyfriend, looks back, but doesn't respond to her screams. His eyes are open yet, he seems just like Michael and the medic! Awake, but so far away from consciousness. He is in even worse shape. His forehead is split open like a smashed melon and blood has run down covering his face. The blood has now dried and caked on covering much of his face.

He groans and jerks aggressively in his seat to free himself from the restraints of the safety belt. Seeing his actions, his girlfriend doesn't waste anymore time. Without delay, she jumps over the rear bench and lands hard on her back in the cargo space. She regains control, reaches the door handle and swings open the cargo door.

The suv is eight feet off the ground. The girl gets down on her stomach and begins to work herself down, stomach first from the pileup. Hearing the commotion at the rear of the suv, Michael and the medic hurry to the sound. Back at the scene of the first wreck, the police officer that was attacked by Michael, he along with another medic begin stumbling towards the girl, as well. Along with the police officer there are three others who were also attacked at the scene. These creatures are following after the officer.

The girl decides now is, as good of time to escape as any. She jumps down to the highway below. Michael and the medic come around the side of the suv to see her standing in a half crouched position wiping at her thighs and hips. The moment she hears the sound of their footsteps running towards her, she takes off on the highway heading back west, the direction she was coming from. The young woman runs in the fourth lane, jumps the concrete divider and enters the west bound lanes of traffic. The westbound lanes are backed up for over a mile, as a result of the chaos in the eastbound lanes.

As, the young woman weaves her way from the fourth lane into the third, right behind her is Michael and the medic as they cross the divider seconds behind her. The police officer and his three followers are back behind Michael about seventy five feet. The frighten girl pounds desperately, on the window of a bright red Mazda Miata. Being occupied by a woman who is in her early forties, the woman is stuck in mile deep traffic. Looking away, the woman does not make eye contact in order not to acknowledge the girl pounding on the window of her car.

Michael and the medic are now within twenty five feet of her, so she abandons the woman as her savior. Without hesitation, she crosses into the second lane and is almost hit by a guy in his Jeep, as he moves from the third lane. He floors the gas in order to get into the second lane, moving ahead only thirty feet. He honks his horn at her yelling at her.

"Hey get the fuck out of the way, you crazy bitch!"

"You have to help me. These guys are tryin' to kill me!"

He quickly stops his Jeep and opens the half door and steps out to the highway.

"Now, what are you talking about? Are you high or somethin'?"

"We have to get the hell out of here now! They are coming and they're all screwed-up looking"

"Where are they? Over there?"

He asks her, pointing in the direction of the two men stumbling towards them. The police officer and his three followers are now flanking their position to the northeast and are coming towards the two from their rear.

"You don't have to worry, I'll go deal with those sons-of-bitches! You wait here!"

"Don't go, they'll get you."

She tries to yell at him not to go, but he's not listening, as he is off on his macho quest to protect the girl. Michael and the medic are now just ten feet from him. Meanwhile, the police officer and his three followers are still moving towards the girl and the Jeep guys rear. They too are now only twenty feet away. The second group's progress is slowed by the sheer amount of damage done by Michael and the female medic when they attacked these four *'new'* creatures.

4

11:45 A.M. October 28, 2006

A St. Louis Metropolitan Police squad car is sitting in the empty parking lot of Gateway Trust on the corner of Manchester and Chouteau. The day has been calm so, far after being on the beat for six hours now. Jackson Barton and Darryl Hopkins have only had two calls. The first being a shoplifting case at the corner market a block before Kingshighway. Simple enough, the shop owner had the would be thief at bay with his 9 mm handgun. A gun the shopkeeper keeps under his register for just these very cases. So, Darryl and Jackson simply grabbed the scared teen and ran him without indict to the city jail which is located Downtown.

The second was a domestic disturbance, involving a seventy three year old African American grandmother and her twenty one year old grandson. The dispute was down to the fact that the grandmother wanted the grandson to move out and a get a job which the grandson did not want to do. Thus a argument insue and the police were called. The outcome the grandson, left the house and promised to move in with friends. Case closed, for now.

Now, both officers are sitting inside of their squad car waiting for a follow-up call from dispatch when over intercom comes the message neither men ever thought they would hear.

"Attention all unit's! Attention all unit's! We have a major civil disturbance on east and westbound lanes of Highway 44. Civil disorder has also been reported on the northbound lanes of Kingshighway Boulevard. At this time, it appears if there is single group responsible for all of these incidents. All available unit's are requested to respond!"

"Damn then, Darryl, lets get going." Says a eager Barton.

With that Darryl flips the siren and lights on motoring off towards the scene.

"Dispatch, this is unit 24, we are heading to the 3200 hundred block of Kingshighway Boulevard, ETA two minutes." Darryl speaks to the shoulder mounted radio.

"Copy 24. Back-up has been requested to assist you." The female dispatcher says.

This stretch of Manchester Avenue is littered with annoying stoplights that turn red the instant you approach them. On this mile stretch of road there is seven of these very lights. The worst aspect of all is on the cross streets from Sarah to Kingshighway. There is no traffic coming except for the sporadic vehicle.

With his screaming sirens and their bright flashing lights, Officers Hopkins and Barton blow through Continental. The Chevrolet engine grunts as Darryl shoves his right foot down on the accelerator. The speedometer rises from thirty five to sixty five in a mere four seconds. Darryl dives to the left hand lane to pass some idiot who does not yield to him. He quickly passes the Nissan Pathfinder and with just inches to spare, dives back to the right lane, inches from the guys bumper.

Now, after passing that idiot all Darryl eyes see are red. He is like a charging bull through Valencia, as his senses take over. He can see moves from lane to lane three, four steps ahead. This is what athletes refer to as being *'in the zone'*. Darryl is just two stoplights from Kingshighway Boulevard now. From his initial speed of he finds even more left in reserve. His speed passes quickly from sixty five to over eighty miles per hour, as he flies through his fifth red light at the intersection of Manchester and Bentley. Now Kingshighway is only a mere quarter mile away from.

But, this quarter mile stretch is home to numerous abandoned homes with various African-American males hanging around the local grocery store. Unbeknownst to the officers is, this is the calm before the storm that is brewing Kingshighway. The outbreak is spreading like a Californian wildfire off of the major thoroughfares of the city and into smaller arteries that feed the intestates their steady diet of local traffic, which is heading either to Highway's 44 or 40. With these two highways they form a complete circle around the entire St. Louis Metropolitan area, that includes a population of more 2.5 million residents. This outbreak could very easily and without delay encircle the city. Also, with how the interstate system is configured in this country it could allow it to spiral through the whole midwestern section of the United States and then from there, where next?

Darryl arrives at Kingshighway and makes a left. It's does not take long for him and Jackson to see the sights of what is happening to the residents of St. Louis. The scene on Kingshighway is total chaos as cars are wrecked in the middle of the road, smoldering on fire while two others dangle over the now cracked retaining wall which is high above the railroad tracks below. The sudden impact resorted in sending both of the vehicles barreling through a foot thick concrete retaining wall. A truck is stuck in the wall and lays there with it's engine bay is on fire. The scene is a surreal to look at and looks as if were filmed for a post apocalyptic movie from the 1980's.

Officer Hopkins slows his speed down to twenty five miles per hour. Both of the officers soak in the sights that their eyes are now witnessing first hand. The two men were here at this very same spot not forty five minutes ago and all was peaceful. Now, not even, an hour later the scene is a disaster zone. Emerging out of a badly wrecked, early 1990's Taurus comes staggering, an elderly man. He is frail and seems disoriented from the impact of the accident. Officer Hopkins quickly weaves his squad car in between the Taurus and the vehicle it smashed into. Barton is facing the elderly man head on, when officer Hopkins stops the vehicle. Jackson Barton opens the door and exit's the car quickly turning on his Motorola chest radio.

"24 to base. We have multiple TA with injuries. Also, back-up is required as we have massive chaos as four cars have breached the retaining wall. We need ambulances and fire support."

"Copy that 24. Back-up is unavailable at this time."

Barton yells over to Hopkins that there will be no back up coming.

"Shit, then I'll go down there and check out what is going on." Says Hopkins.

"Fine, I'll take care of this scene here!"

Barton replies and with that Hopkins reenters his squad car and drives towards the scene of the cars that have broken through the retaining walls. While Hopkins attends to the accident a half mile down Kingshighway. Barton moves his attend to the older gentleman.

"Are you doin' all right?"

There is no response from the man and he appears really disoriented. Then he stumbles and falls hard against his detached front bumper. Officer Barton, quick as a puma, jumps over the front of the wrecked Taurus in an attempt to catch the obviously injured man. The moment, Barton arrives at the footstep of the elderly gentleman, he springs to life. Barton is so surprised by the man's reverse in condition, he falls backwards on his just pressed pant bottom.

Then the old man emits a primal scream that is extremely freaky. As, Barton tries to react, the old man lunges quickly towards him. Desperate to get back to his feet, Barton side steps the old man and he crashes into the side of the second car. The old man comes at him again. This time though Barton pulls out his collapsible metal nightstick from his utility belt. From out his mouth, he questions what in the hell the old man is doing. If, Officer Barton was seeking the old man to provide some clarity on his actions, he isn't providing any. The air around them is full of black smoke from two of the vehicles on fire that pierced the retaining wall.

When Officer Hopkins left his partner to help out, he passed by many vehicles, and it doesn't take very long for him to figure out there are no survivors. The impact and damage is tremendous. No way could anyone have lived through such an impact. Back on his own, Officer Barton swings the club at the old man.

SMACK! The hard metal club hit's and tears it's way into the soft wrinkled flesh of the old man's back. The flesh around the wound burst opens and immediately, you can see the flesh visible through his light blue polo shirt. But, yet again no blood is coming to the surface of the old man's wound. The powerful shot doesn't stop the man from attacking at Officer Barton again. This time, the old man charges for Barton's legs, but the lightweight frame of the man is nowhere near enough to knock the well-built, solid frame of St. Louis Police Officer Jackson Barton down.

Barton reaches down to the old man, grabbing him around the armpit and lifts him with little effort. He lifts the light, 110-pound frail man and slams him up against the front of the man's Taurus. In one quick motion, he flips the man's hands behind his back and slaps the handcuffs on his bony left wrist. Next the right wrist goes into the tightly locked metal cuffs.

Once cuffed, he slams the lightweight man face first against the damaged passenger side door of the Ford Taurus. The old man falls down to the ground instantly, but even down on the ground with his hands behind his back. He still tries to fight his way back to his feet. Struggling on the ground he tries to get back to his feet. The old man is flip-flopping like a fish out of water on the greasy, oily asphalt of Kingshighway. Barton takes the thick rubber sole of his Caterpillar boot and knocks the old man temporarily on his butt, but that does not keep the old man still for long. As, the officer looks down at the old man in a bewildered look.

"I don't know what the fuck is wrong with you old man, but you better damn bet your ass is going to be spending time in the city jail!"

The old man does not react or respond to what has just been said to him. Tired of messing around with the old man and his difficulties. He reaches down and yanks the man up like a bag of feathers. The sharp steel of the cuffs dig into the elderly man's soft loose fresh. A small amount of blood creeps out from around where the cuffs dug into him and drops unseen to the ground.

With the man under his control in just one hand, Barton is forced to improvise and opens the right rear door to the old man's Taurus. With little effort throws the man inside. As, soon as the man is inside of the car, Barton slams the door on the car and pauses beside the trunk. Collecting himself, Barton now gets on his chest radio and calls to his partner, who is still down attending to the four T.A.'s at the bridge.

"Barton to Hopkins, you there?"

"Yeah, I'm down here. It's not good. There are no survivors. So, far I've pulled eight bodies out. It's real bad and there are four more cars I haven't even gotten to yet. Over."

"Darryl, you have to come back here and see what I got. The old man I pulled out of the TA, out of nowhere he went loco on me. So, I slammed his ass with the cuffs and threw him in his car. He's still going crazy in the back seat. You gotta see him back here, Darryl."

Darryl's voice comes over Barton's speaker.

"Yeah, Barton I'll be back to you in less than two minutes."

"I'll be waitin' for you here, so will the old geezer." Barton replied.

Darryl comes walking from his squad car. He is surprised at the damage from the four TA's he attended. The look plastered on his face tells the story of what he has endured in these past ten minutes. One would be correct in believing that Officer Hopkins is nothing but pissed-off!

"What the hell is this all this about, Barton? It better be worth my time coming all the way back here!"

Barton, sure his yarn will impress his partner.

"You have to check out this nut, he just freaked out on me when I approached his car. I don't have a damn clue what the fuck his deal is."

Darryl along with Barton walk from beside their squad car towards the Taurus. The old man who after all of this, is still putting up a struggle in the back seat of the Ford sedan.

"See what you make of this loon."

Darryl leaves his partner and walks closer to have a look at what is really going on in the back seat. Barton remains behind Darryl about four to five feet. Step by step, he is now within earshot and hears a strange noise emitting from the back of the car. He cannot quite distinguish yet, what it is and how a man could make such a noise. The old man kicks violently at the window. He then slams his body against the door, but still there is no escape. Darryl picks up on this as he approaches the car.

His body position becomes much more guarded. He is now viewing one of the strangest sights that, he has ever seen in his fourteen years on the job. He picks up immediately that, the old man does not seem to be awake in our world. The man is so disoriented as he repeatedly, violently slams his body against the car's interior. Darryl is standing just at an arms length from the old man but in terms of humanity they could not be further apart from each other.

Within moments of seeing the actions of the man, Darryl yells over to Barton.

"What's wrong with this old guy? What, do you think he's on something? What could he possibly be on?"

He doesn't look at his partner when he asks the questions and he doesn't look back to see for his reply either. Darryl knows nothing can explain the man's strange behavior.

"Hell, if I know Darryl. Maybe he forgot his meds. Like I said when I called you over here, he just came out of his car like a wild mustang. He's the craziest damn guy I have ever put down, that's for sure!"

"I just can't figure this all out, Barton. There's got to be more to this."

"What the hell are you talking about Darryl?"

"You don't think it's odd? We're getting all these strange calls. It's doesn't add up. Think about it, Barton. Dispatch said a major civilian disorder but when we show-up all that is here is this old fart and four TA's. Things just aren't adding up."

His partner is not as philosophical as, he is and does not get the gist of what his mind is analyzing. Barton is a bright enough guy but he is not the kind of person who seeks the meaning of things. If, he doesn't know it, then he never will. More importantly he doesn't care too, either.

Darryl is much more analytical and educated. He graduated from the University of Missouri at St. Louis (UMSL) with a degree in Criminal Justice. His wife of the past nine years is a tenth grade high school science teacher in Edwardsville, Illinois. Her name is Sofia. They met in college during the fall semester of 1995. The two had so much in common that their relationship grew and progressed rapidly. They were married in just a mere ten months.

Fast forward in time nine years and their relationship is like the gorgeous white cliffs of Dover. Sophia means the world to her husband and vise-versa. Right now, he would rather be lying in bed next to her like they do every Sunday morning 'till noon. But, he isn't lying next to her. He is slap in the center of Kingshighway dealing with a situation that he can't quite get a handle on. He wonders what's going to happen with a partner doesn't seem to grasp the seriousness of the situation at hand.

"So, what do you think we should do, Darryl?"

Darryl drops his head down and looks at the ground below him as, if the ground will speak to him and tell him the answers. He does not find the answer from the tarmac below but from his own mind.

"We need to go further south down Kingshighway to find what the source of this report is."

Barton is eager for any new challenge and he gung-ho agrees with Darryl.

"Then hell let's go and we'll deal with this crazy old man later!"

With both men in total and complete agreement, the two officers grab the old man from his car and transfer him into their squad car. They begin their journey weaving the Chevrolet Lumina through the broken off bit's of fenders, shattered glass and other smaller pieces of car parts that litter this stretch of Kingshighway now. What is it that Darryl and Barton will find on the Southern side of Kingshighway? What will the results be when they witness the sights? Will they comprehend what they are seeing? What will their actions be then? Will they honor their sworn duty or will their human faults overcome their best intentions?

11:49 A.M. October 28, 2006

Overhead a KEJK traffic copter is thundering overhead and closing in quickly towards the accident scene on the highway. The traffic reporter was tipped off by the MODOT traffic cameras, which are located throughout the highway system in Missouri. The pilot is about a mile from the scene when the camera operator checks through his high powdered lens. His eye is first drawn to the accident scene with Michael's van lying off from the highway.

On the highway, the scene is even more shocking to him. Several large puddles of blood are located where, Michael attacked the medic, but there's an even bigger spot where the police officer was attacked. The cameraman notices a white substance is intermixed among the crimson ooze. His eye narrows in on the open barrel, it's contents is being picked up by the strong gusts of wind whipping down from the helicopter. He rotates the base of the camera to see what is happening in on the west bound lanes.

Philip Roland, the programmer back at KEJK, which is located Downtown St. Louis decides, he needs to interrupt the usual fluff news piece that dominates the national and local news programming these days. Philip allows the cameraman from the helicopter full access to the stations airwaves. Finally, the cameraman's voice cuts over the airwaves.

"This is James Pickfield with KEJK News 'Copter 5. We're on Highway 44 over the Kingshighway exit, where there has been a horrific accident. It appears that a cargo van has crashed into a second vehicle and in the process fell off of the exit ramp. The van is lying, mangled on it's side. We can report that ambulances and emergency personnel are on the scene, but right now there is no movement on the ground at this time. Traffic for the ride home is going to be a long one this afternoon, as traffic is grid locked for two miles already. You'll need to add allow atleast an extra ninety minutes to your commute home We will update you as the situation warrants. Now back to you in the studio."

Though James sent the story back to the studio, his visuals continue to be beamed into everyone in St. Louis home that is tuned in. While James pursues what is really happening down below. He has been a traffic reporter for the last eleven years and has reported on thousands of stories, but for some reason this one feels much different than others. James adjusts the camera lens and takes a wide shot of the backup. He then begins to focus his lens on the developing scuffle that is set to begin between the Jeep driver and the two creatures.

At the extreme left corner of his 3.5" color viewfinder, James witnesses the police officer and his followers emerging and moving towards both, the girl and the Jeep driver. He is shocked when he notices the extent of the medic, police officer his followers and Michael's injuries. If, he was shocked by the sights, it is nothing compared to the state of confusion that is running through Joan Bennett's brain as she sits watching TV in her Compton Heights living room.

Joan is startled by the images and jumps to her feet, yet still remains staring at the images splashing across her TV. Panicked, she yells for her granddaughter to come in and watch this. The signal that is being beamed through their cable line shows Michael and the medic confronting the Jeep driver. The driver singles out Michael and strikes him in the jaw with a powerful right fist. Michael falls to the ground on the cold wet asphalt. Blind sided, the male medic lunges for the driver and brings him down to his knees.

Michael, meanwhile slithers behind the driver and bites down into his leg.

Michael's teeth puncture through the light khaki pants, the driver screams out in horrible pain. Desperately, he kicks violently to get away from his attacker. His first kick misses but the second one is right on. Michael falls back down but is quickly back up. Coming at the driver again, as the medic jumps from behind on top of his back. The medic and Michael emit this strange piercing sound. It's primal in nature, raw and explosive. But, absolutely no way is it human. Yet, the scream for life that the driver lets out is uniquely human. It's the driver's last stand, as now the police officer and his followers are only five feet away and closing in quickly. The driver manages to throw off the medic from his back and he is now limping from the bite that penetrated deep into his thigh. As, well as the deep bite on his traipses muscle which is now bleeding badly. His once dark blue button up shirt is now stained with vividly bright blood. Now, as five of these *'things'* are encircling him. The driver is faced with the horrible situation of being literally eaten alive, by his fellow man.

6

11:51 A.M. October 28, 2006

Joan and Constance Bennett are both glued to their TV set. This is defiantly *'must see'* TV. Nothing either of them have ever witnessed has prepared these two for the sights that they are witnessing first hand.

"What is happening? Why are they so messed-up?"

"I have no idea, dear. I can't believe this isn't some kind of media stunt." Her grandmother adds.

"You call your brother Constance. Call him right now!"

Back on Highway 44 Michael, the medic and two of his followers, continue their attack on the driver. Quickly, the three creatures swarm in on him with pinpoint and brutal precision in their ferociousness. The driver's flesh is ripped open like a fish being gutted. The besieged man screams a bloodcurdling cry into the crisp fall air. The motorists who are witnessing first hand these events, panic and attempt to get from this horrific scene. The drivers panic and slam their bumpers into their neighbor's front and rear ends. Burning tires quickly fill the fall air with a thick cloud of smoke permeating the air with the nauseating smell of burning rubber.

But, for those who are too far back, stuck in mile after mile of traffic, they are blind to what is happening ahead of them. Located a mile west of the Kingshighway exit is Renee Andrews, who just got on 44 from the Shrewsbury exit. Renee is returning from a interesting launch, she just had with her mother at the Red Lobster. After the joy of being told what she's doing wrong and how she should be running her life for the past seventy five minutes, she needed a much deserved break from her reality. Deciding to take the long way home So, she rounded Murdoch Avenue and with reluctance entered onto the highway. The reluctance comes from the realization that in just ten minutes, she would be back home trapped within her regular life. But, for now her journey has been delayed longer than she would have wished for.

She sits impatient in her pale green Accord listening to her usual radio station. Yet, she can't help from zoning out as the barrage of commercials bores her into a dream like haze. As Renee, sits in her car wishing she was anywhere but stuck here in traffic this horrible and annoying noise blares through her car speakers.

EEEHHH!!! EEEHHH!!! EEEHHH!!!

A strange and awful noise and then a very calm and monotone voice begins to speak.

"What the hell is this?" Says Renee to herself.

"This is a message from the Emergency Alert System. From St. Louis, Missouri. This is not a test. This message is for the residents of the following areas of the listening area: St. Louis City, St. Louis County, and St. Clair County in East St. Louis. The Mayor of St. Louis City along with the elected officials of the affected areas have declared a State of Emergency. Also implemented is a curfew set-to begin at 2:00 P.M. Central Standard Time. This order will be enforced fully by law enforcement.

A State of Emergency has been called due to uncontrollable mass civil violence and disobedience through out the entire affected areas. At this time, there is no explanation for this wide spread mass violence. Government officials have arrested some of the attackers, but at this time there is no further information on what to look out for.

There are unconfirmed reports of extremely injured individuals carrying out these attacks. But, these are unconfirmed and we do not any confirmation as to their motives. The attackers do not appear to be looting after an attack, but the numbers appear to show some kind of semi organized mass riot across the St. Louis Metropolitan area.

As of 11:52 A.M., a State of Emergency has been enacted. All residents in the affected areas are ordered by the chief of police to return to your homes and then not to leave until the situation is brought under control. Anyone caught violating curfew will be arrested and charged. Anyone attempting to loot during this time will be shoot without warning. This act of emergency is in effect 'till further notice."

"This is the end of the Emergency Alert Message...."

"Oh, fucking great!" Renee shouts, as all semblance of order breaks down and pandemonium sets in.

In unison all of those who are in the left hand lane take to the grass to avoid, whatever it is the government has ordered a State of Emergency over. The level panic and fear is obvious as people take horrible actions in haste. This section of the city is quite hilly with huge granite boulders in which the highway was cut through. One additional fact is that the angle is very steep and for those driving vehicles with low ground clearance it spells trouble, for those who seek to escape.

A young male driving a Toyota sedan comes onto the embankment too fast and loses control of his vehicle. Instantly, the vehicle slides uncontrollable sideways. The sedan continues to slides for more than twenty feet before stopping, as it hits a huge boulder. The car flips on it's passenger right side before finally ending on it's roof. The boy inside is tossed about roughly inside the interior. The bright yellow Camry comes to a stop, as it is tangled in a chain link fence. As, well as a couple of small trees. The others, who were luckier than the Camry, scoot by and speed off on a near by neighborhood street. The teen lies inside of his car bloody and badly injured, yet not a single person passing by is authoring any help to the teen.

Back on Highway 44, at the Kingshighway exit, the driver from the Jeep is down on the ground and putting up no defense at all. Michael out of the five creatures seems to be taking great pleasure and pride in destroying this person. Do these *'things'* think in a vindictive way? It sure seems that way as Michael gnaws on the flesh of the Jeep drivers arm with all the zeal of an Islamic extremist.

The police officer and one of his creatures pursue the young girl. The terrified girl tries to run around a Imo's Pizza truck to escape from these two. But, they are one step ahead of her. They flank the two ends of the truck to meet up at the front of the delivery truck. When the girl sees the hungered creature in front of her, she quickly turns around then realizes that the police officer is coming towards her from the back of the truck. It's in this moment, she realizes that escaping from the two creatures is impossible. For, she has seen first hand the physical damage these *'things'* do. The creatures run towards the fear stricken woman and arrive to her in only three big steps. She drops to her knees out of fear the instant before they arrive at her. Instead of coming at her face level, the creatures tackle her down to the ground. Once down on the ground, they swarm the defensive less girl, as they swallow her whole.

The girl's back is slammed hard against the roadway, knocking her unconscious. The police officer moves in and with it's ravaged mouth bites out a mouthful of the unconscious woman's cheek. Two huge squirts of blood, shoots everywhere from her massive wound. The pain is too much for even the deep unconsciousness of the woman to ignore. The sensors which regulate this can not hold under it's spell any longer. They scream for her to wake up.

She does come out of unconsciousness and returns to this world with her lungs in full scream. The police officer returns for a second feeding opportunity and rips through the thin first layer of skin on her neck. Even more massive quantities of blood come bubbling up to the surface pouring from the girls neck. Then finally, down her chest. The quantity of blood from the ragged wound is so great that within seconds it begins to pour on the roadway. With the traumatic force to her throat, she takes one last gargling breath of what was her young life. But, even with her passing from this world, that doesn't stop the feeding frenzy as the creatures dig deep into dead woman's flesh. The secondary ghoul tears into the stomach area through her latest in-style blouse and enters directly into her stomach area.

After witnessing the horrific events to not only the defenseless girl but everyone else through this high powered wide angle lens. James Pickfield orders the pilot to turn the craft to the north and bring the helicopter closer to the scene. He knows that this is the biggest news story he will ever break, with that knowledge, he is brimming with excitement. The pilot breaks to the northwest and comes in quickly to hover above the scene. James's camera never for even a single second misses one image from this developing catastrophe.

With the chaos happening around them, the other motorists flee from their automobiles in terror. It is quite a abnormal site, to see thousands of people abandoning their cars and scattering in every possible direction over the lanes of a major highway. Sensing new prey, the creatures lunge after the motorists with the efficiency of a crocodile lying in surprise for a gazelle. Throughout all of this, James manages to keep his 35 millimeter lens focused on the sights, as person after person, life is taken by these vicious creatures. What are the people of St. Louis witnessing this live on TV, thinking is difficult to imagine.

Shock, horror and disbelief. Are the first three things which come to mind. What in the world could be the cause of this shocking and brutal mass murdering? Must be another. And why are the creatures eating the people they attack? Also in back of their minds has to be; how far will this escalate to and am I next?

7

11:53 P.M. October 28, 2006

Directly, under the overpass are four soaked creatures walking towards, the four city workers. To a passerby, this unavoidable confrontation looks drastically one sided. The creatures gained incredible physical strength and the lack of compassion. They only believe in the gift of eternal life after death. The battle is just seconds from beginning and the odds are now stacking up quickly against the workers. Jay, a burly white fellow sounds off with one last verbal jab before the violence begins.

If, this an attempt scare off the creatures or if he is using this to psyche himself and his coworkers before the unavoidable battle. It seems to be working on his coworkers. They're getting pumped up and appear ready for the fight. However, it has no effect on the approaching creatures. The driver of the truck is armed with an eighteen inch steel pipe takes the lead with the tall slim black passenger, just steps behind. The creatures feel no fear, they just stumble towards the city workers. There's no yelling, or hurry to their movements. There is complete silence except for an occasional moan from their lifeless mouths.

The terrified woman from the highway takes cover along the side of the city work truck. The north bound lane of traffic is clogging up. The drivers are honking their horns and yelling for the men to get back in their trucks. Sparing all them the hassle of sitting in traffic for an extra five minutes. The workers ignore the noise from the traffic. What's more important to society? Helping someone in distress or driving to load up on burgers filled with high cholesterol from a fast food establishment?

It's obvious from the response of the drivers what their choice is. Unfortunately, this attitude is not uncommon. The older generation always comments that *'this'* new generation, people are too fast paced, self absorbed. They lack the sense to care and are not interested in the well beings of their neighbors and others. This may be true, I cannot say for sure. I'am not immortal, yet from my life experiences, I would have to politely disagree. I believe that people only care about the little world in which they have insulated for themselves.

It is always said, I don't want to get involved but, today is different. The plague has exploded and is destroying St. Louis. Everyday people, whether rich or poor, black or white, man or woman will be forced not only to get along but help their fellow man. This is their only hope for survival from the gaining firestorm of the living dead.

Without warning, the pipe smashes into the left temple of the lead male ghoul. The creature is stunned and staggers backwards. Though the blow left a gaping hole in his left temple, there is no blood, from the impact. The ghoul's temple opens up, but still there is no blood coming to the surface. Before the man can process that information, he is jumped by a male creature and the female medic.

The female hit's him low. He struggles to regain it's balance. Yet, falls down to the slick roadway. Simultaneously, the male creature hit's him in the stomach. The city worker grabs the creature around the gut and flips it over onto it's back. The ghoul hit's the asphalt hard, but gets right back up like a rubber bouncy ball from a vending machine.

Things are not going to be any better for the other three men. The huge city worker takes his wrench and begins to beat down on this thin, pale blonde creature. The first hit, is an outrageously hard smash. Followed up a mere instant latter with an equally hard smack to the forehead that rips open it's nose at the bridge. You can see the cartilage pop out of the skin. For some unknown reason, no blood at all comes to the surface or spills on the face of the creatures. It's as if the creature's blood no longer flows to the various parts of their almost lifeless bodies.

A third blow lands on the back of it's head. The ghoul, under relentless attack, falls to it's hands and knees. The creature's brown tweed pants are ripped at both knees and along the side of the left thigh. The man delivers a fourth blow to the small of the back. The ghoul hits the ground chest first, but again begins to get up. Surprised that the creature isn't damn near death, the city worker drops the heavy wrench on the once busy city street. Instead, he begins to kick the ghoul with his size 11 steal toed boot.

BAMM! Kick one is delivered to the stomach and a second kick breaks three of the creature's ribs. The sound is unmistakable as the relentless city worker is encouraged by the distinct sound a broken bone makes. The third kick is delivered to the ghoul's mouth. Out pop four teeth, but still it does not bleed. The ghoul jumps right back to it's feet. The worker is shocked and cannot believe this is happening to him. The creature grabs the large shoulders of the man and in one beat of the man's heart.

It takes it's remaining teeth and rips into the soft flabby flesh that exists around the worker's neck. It's teeth go deep into the skin as they enter into the fatty substance that exists underneath the epidermis. Blood pops to the surface and the huge hulking city worker falls heavily to the ground. The creature continues it's attack. The blood flows from the man like that of the Mississippi River that runs just three miles from Kingshighway.

8

12:05 P.M. October 28, 2006

One can only wish and pray that those people who are down on the riverfront at Laclede's Landing taking in all the tourist sights the city has to offer. Such sights, as the world famous, St. Louis Arch and the renovated beautiful Riverfront area of town. In addition there are those having a nice early fall lunch at one of the many restaurant down on The Landing. These people only know that today, October 28, is a beautiful crisp fall day and no doubt are quite pleased that the long hot summer days are over. For the time being, the nice cool fall weather is here. But, an eerie feel has began to descend across the city. The TV is broadcasting live footage from a news helicopter, of the horrors on Highway 44.

The breaking news report plays in many of the bar and restaurant's TV set's. The volume is muted but the closed caption is on. The words go from left to right across the 27" screens.

"A major civil unrest has broke out on Highway 44, we have confirmed reports of people physically being attacked and killed. At this time we do not yet know the nature of the attacks. It does not seem to be in any organized patterns. So far the incidents have been reported on the eastbound lanes of Highway 44 at the Kingshighway exit. In addition, we have had several reports at this location also with incidents at Kingshighway and Chippewa. Lastly, we have reports of violent attacks taking place as far away as Kingshighway and Manchester. The police are not commenting as to the extent of the civil disobedience. There is no further information as to what, if any, precautions residents of the St. Louis Metropolitan area should take. When updates are announced, we will pass them along to you."

Unfortunately, none of the many patrons eating lunch at any of these establishments happen to be paying much attention to the words that are going across the screen. Even if they did, nearly every report differs on the situation. For, those who are viewing these images, they appear to be nothing more than meaning less ways to pass the time during their lunch hour. Most of the viewers probably think it's one of those countless reality programming that are beginning to dominate the programming lineup on cable stations like F/X and Spike TV. Tragically for the patrons and home viewers, the warning goes unnoticed. For now, they are spared from the horror that is taking place in the South side of St. Louis.

9

12:07 P.M. October 28, 2006

Now, with two of their fellow comrades down, the physical intensity level as well as the sense of desperation is beginning to set in and overcome the two remaining city workers. As they continue to battle these indestructible creatures. With unwavering determination the four creatures encircle the two outnumbered men. The two remaining men look each other in the eye. They know they face an enormous uphill struggle in combating these creatures. Up to this point, the men have hit them with everything they have and the damage done to the creatures is immense, but still they show absolutely no signs of slowing down or stopping their attack on the men.

"What the hell are we going to do, Ray?"

"Hit the sons-of-bitches!"

Is the reply to John Robinson, who is the youngest at twenty three years old and has only been working for the city for only the last seven months. John lives in North City on Delmar. John wastes no time swinging and hit's the stumbling Vietnamese creature in the stomach with one of the heavy steel pipes that the workers use in the field. The impact forces the creature to slump down to it's hands and knees, but the creature pops quickly back in place. John swings for a second time and hits the ghoul this time directly in the head, it's scalp split's open. He does not waste time as he hit's the ghoul with two more quick strikes to the temple region. The jarring impact shocks the light-framed ghoul, but still it does not stop the creature. Now the female medic from the highway, who was chasing the woman joins the fray as well.

She hits John in the back and with the Vietnamese ghoul they both force John down to the roadway. He continues trying to fight with all he has, to frantically get the creatures off of him, as quick as possible. He strikes at them with his bare fists abandoning the steel pipe which falls to the roadside. He tries with every bit of life left in his lanky body, but the two creatures vicious onslaught is much too much for him or anyone else. There's nothing anyone can do against the creatures. The female medic bites down deep into his mid-thigh, right through his dark midnight blue Dickie's work pants. Profoundly, deep she drives her teeth into his thigh as John screams in agonizing terror.

She returns for a second helping and the Vietnamese creature strikes John at his neck. The creature returns back up ripping a two-inch chunk of flesh from his body. Although the creatures teeth are not sharp enough to pierce through his tough skin, the creature jerks violently pulling the skin to it's breaking point. But, it doesn't sit idly by for long instead, it dives back in biting down on the same wounded piece of flesh. This time it's teeth go through the tough skin. The blood flows freely out of John's neck and down on his lifeless shoulders. The pair of creatures does not stop their attack there, even though he shows no signs of life as he falls down to the ground. They continue to rip deep into flesh, on the body that once was John Robinson.

The damage done by the pair is quite extensive as John's right leg above the knee is missing most of the flesh that once made up a normal thigh. John's throat and neck suffered more damage than the German Panzer divisions did during World War Two. The Vietnamese creature did a number on the throat and neck areas. His throat is missing a two inch chunk of flesh which was ripped off, as well as two other jagged holes. Which, together now form one single wound. The roadway is soaked with the plasma of the man. While John faced death and ultimately did just that, Ray has his own troubles with the unstoppable creatures. The two which were not attacking John were battling with him. He decided early on from what he saw from Billy and John is that there is almost no way to overcome them physically, so he decides he needs to out smart these, senseless creatures. He hip tosses the pale thin blonde guy that Billy beat down.

Billy took his four pound Craftsman wrench and broke three of this ghoul's ribs and even now the creature comes full force at Ray. He pushes the creature in the back, as it was charging him. It falls down but moves right back to it's knees. Just as, he disposes of one without delay he's got a second creature to deal with. This one steps right in line to take the first ones place. This creature is in it's mid-sixties, a white male wearing those stereotypical, thin light blue cotton trousers that it seems like every man over the age of fifty five wears.

The elderly creature grabs a hold of Ray's biceps and clamps down. Quickly, he turns to the left to shake the lightweight creature off of his arm before it bites any further. But, the creature's grip on his biceps is viselike and it's feet come up off the road two feet. Seeing that this is useless, he decides, he has to change his tactics. Ray stops spinning and the creature falls to the ground. He punches at it's stomach and finally it's grip is broken. But, then the rail thin creature comes lunging for him again. The ghoul hit's Ray in the lower stomach and his lungs empty from the impact. He struggles to regain his breath where he can fight back against these two creatures. He quickly pushes the thin creature down on the ground, then headhunts the older one.

He grabs a hold of his arm and swings the creature and then when the momentum is just enough, he sling shots the old ghoul on to Kingshighway. He lets go and away the ghoul goes. Ray is by no means a stupid guy and he knows like any good gambler at one of the many casinos on Laclede's Landing, when it's time to leave, it's time to leave! Get out while you are still ahead. He jumps halfway over the hood of a young African American woman's early 1990's Ford Escort. Landing hard on the thin metal hood, the lady angrily jumps up and with hand and head gestures to him, she shows just how unpleased she is with his actions. She then sticks her head out of her driver's side window to yell at him, he is now past her car and on his way back to his truck.

"You fat muther-fucka, your fat ass dented up my car!"

Ray offers no reply in order to fuel the woman's raging anger and in truth he never even heard anything the woman had to say. He was too focused on getting to the women from the highway and then getting out of this hell zone.

"Hey! Hurry the hell up and get in the truck! We gotta get the hell outta here!" Ray yells to the woman.

"What about them?" She replies in a somber tone to him.

"Fuck them, let's get out of here before…"

He is interrupted by the two of the creatures. The female medic and the reed thin creature, who comes running towards both him and his truck. The creatures are quick and it doesn't take either of the two, long to realize that now is *'THE'* time to move and later would be the correct time to ask any questions you might have. Ray, without hesitation, opens the chrome door handle and with the door swinging open, he takes one big step on the ladder board and lands on the air cushioned drivers seat. The woman also finds herself quickly opening the heavy orange door and in even less time, she slams the door closed. Just as quickly, she cranks the window closed and locks the door. Ray, at the same time starts up the diesel engine and releases the clutch and away the Freightliner Business Class M2 sputters away.

Smashing into a parked Ford van that the driver left abandoned to see what all the commotion was about. Ray glances over quickly at the woman, who is staring straight ahead, north onto Kingshighway. He can see that she is physically fine but emotionally, not doing so well. With one last look in his driver's side mirror he, views the four creatures swarming the remaining cars of those who have not yet gotten out of their destructive path. With that last look at the horrible scene, he turns his eyes toward the road ahead. What lies ahead for him and his new passenger? What is their fate? And the bigger subtext is what is the fate of St. Louis and it's people? The answer to those questions is one in the same and unbeknownst to them both and the city, as well is there is not one. They both are living on time that is quickly evaporating away.

10

12:09 P.M. OCTOBER 28, 2006

The location is the Benton Park neighborhood, a nice suburban retreat in the middle of a chaotic city. Located in southern section of town, directly off the major artery of Grand Boulevard. Highway 44 is located just a half mile to their north. Inside of the early 1920's home are Joan and Constance Bennett who are both still in disbelief at the events they are watching live on their living room television set.

From over the airwaves comes further updates on the panic happening all around the city and county.

"This in from our field reporters on the scene in Des Peres, we are receiving word that the lines at the gas pumps are swamped with residents fearful of this outbreak. We have also had hundreds of calls alerting us that lines at the areas banks and ATM's are a scene of chaos. We ask that everyone listening, please exercise good common sense and not to over react." A second newscaster interrupts.

"Yes, what we don't need at this time is for our emergency personnel, to have to divert their attention away from the outbreak for minor situations."

"What do you make of this Grandma?"

"I'm not sure Constance, it looks like those people just went completely insane. It's hard to know what crazy people are thinking."

Joan tells Constance her granddaughter in a effort to calm the late teenage girl down.

"It makes me more than a little worried, Grandma Kingshighway is only a mile and a half down 44."

She says in reply. You can tell the images of the extreme carnage are starting to wear and tear on her nerves.

"What will we do if it spreads here?" She is growing more rapid with her erratic questions.

"Calm down, Constance. This is just some isolated incident. The police will have it handled in a matter of minutes. I am sure of that dear."

Joan's reassurances have the desired effect on her and are evident in Constance's vocal reply.

"Yeah, I guess you're right about that, Grandma."

She walks out of the living room into the tile-floored kitchen. She shouts to where her grandmother can hear her from the split rooms.

"I am making a Swiss and turkey sandwich. Grandma, do you know where the good mustard is?"

Seemingly, forgetting her hesitation and dismay of just two minutes ago.

"In the pantry, where the spare food always is."

You can tell by Joan's pitch and tone in her voice this is not the first time she has had to tell her granddaughter where to find, what she is looking for.

"Why, don't you go ahead make me half a sandwich as well?" She laughs a little chuckle.

"What was that, Grandma?"

Constance asks her grandmother even though she really heard her question. Right now, she just doesn't really want to be bothered to make her grandmother a sandwich.

"Oh, nothing dear, don't worry about it."

She says with a laugh and then sits back down in her Art Deco style high back chair and presses the power button on her remote control to turn off the television set. Joan flicks her overhead, Tiffany lamp that she purchased all the way back in the summer of '37 on. Reaching down she picks up the book, that she has been trying to finish for the past two weeks. Yet, she's been so busy with the Tower Grove Park Association board meetings that she hasn't been able to, so. Two meetings a week in addition to all the extra time spent talking on the telephone to various members and drawing in potential new recruit's. All of these distractions has had a adverse effect on her reading time.

"Boy, it's good to finally have a second off to myself with some calm. It's really nice, that's for sure." Joan says to herself in her usual quiet soft voice.

11

12:11 P.M. OCTOBER 28, 2006

Sitting in her cubicle on the eighth floor at St. Louis University Hospital. Claretha Philps is finally getting in the flow of things at work today following her lunch break. Key after key is struck, logging information on the hospital's computer. She enters the amount of payments made from the patients and their insurance companies against their accounts. She receives any remaining balance left over and forwards it to the account representatives down in collections.

Nancy Williams, who occupies the cubicle next to her has her mini-Magnavox radio tuned on her usual light pop radio station 104.1, The Gateway. This is one of these stations that play the forgettable pop hit's of the day, featuring bands like The Goo Goo Dolls and Rob Thomas. In addition the DJ's promote the hot at the moment trendy bar's who cater to happy hour seekers. Where many of the cites over worked secretaries can get cheap drinks, while the over paid and over sexed lawyers, accountants and stockbrokers try their best to impress these underpaid and generally screwed over women. The men here say all the things in their pitch for the ladies attention they believe a woman wants to hear from them. Ranging from how much money they make or how much power they have to what possessions they have in their lives.

Any women who has attended more than two of these social experiments are quite wise to their game. Within ten seconds of meeting these guys, the experienced lady can tell, what it is these guys are looking for. For example, you have the serial monogamist. Everyone knows this type of guy, he goes from one serious relationship and then when that one is over, he jumps right into another serious relationship without any down time at all.

The second type of guy is the most common. The one-night stand guy, they come on, to the woman extremely aggressively and press their credentials until the girl caves in from the sheer overwhelmness of everything. Or, she falls for his lines of bullshit. Or possibly it's just the fact the woman says to herself.

"Hell, maybe if I fuck him he'll shut his mouth for a moment. Maybe…"

Is the thinking of the wiser type of woman. Finally, the last kind of guy is the shy type. He would never go up to one of the girls, even if his life depended on it. This is either a result from one bad experience too many or simply the fact that he is misogynistic. Harboring a deep fear and hatred of woman. Or maybe somewhere in the middle of the two. So, any girl who believes that dollar drinks are a great deal, it must be her first day on the job.

The afternoon DJ Jim Rollins comes in while the last note is ending.

"It seems we have a breaking news bulletin from the KEJK News 'Copter 5. The reports coming in are more than a little strange to say the least…"

Not intended to be broadcast. "Is this some kind of joke?"

A distant shout from the background of The Gateway's studio in a hurried voice from the switch board operator.

"No, just read it!"

"All right everyone, this is a very bizarre situation for me now. Based on confirmed reports from the St. Louis Metropolitan Police Department and also from KEJK News, there is an infection that is spreading to people in the St. Louis listening area. So far, the unknown infection is reportedly causing mass violence to those which become infected with this yet still unknown virus. The main areas of the infection zone lies off of Highway 44."

"Still more reports place the outbreak directly on Highway 44 in both east and west bound lanes. So, far we have confirmed fatalities on 94 men, woman and children…"

The DJ gives a pause before he begins his next report.

"Also, we have some sporadic reports of the same type of violence in the Hampton Village Shopping Mall. As, well confirmed reports of five killed in the Carondelet neighborhood in the Southern edge of St. Louis City."

"The Mayor of St. Louis George Mays and Police Chief Frank Klostermann have ordered a 24-hour state of emergency including a curfew that starts at 2:30 pm central time. So far, the attackers appear to attack in groups of three or more. At this time, we have very few details on what type of symptoms to look for. The attackers do not appear to speak to their victims, before they attack. In addition, many of the attackers appear to be heavily injured."

The horrified DJ takes a moment for himself in order take all of this new information in and tries to find a way to process it.

"Until we receive more information, we ask that everyone listening right now please use extreme caution and stay in your homes or place of business. Until we receive further word which we will immediately pass onto you as soon as we have it. We ask that you do not try and take to the roads to see for yourselves these events. This situation is very dangerous right now."

Claretha Philps jumps out of her swivel chair and stands up to witness six other of her fellow data processors looking around the office at each other dumbfounded as well. Each not really knowing what to think or what to do. It's like that strange unknown and empty feeling most of us felt that 11th day of September, when the twin 110 story towers collapsed into massive piles of rubble.

The woman whose radio alerted them all to the calamity, happening a mere three quarters of a mile away from them speaks up.

"What should we do? I can't believe what's going on!"

The six women start talking amongst themselves, quickly the conversation goes from being a semi-calm discussion. Then the moment when no definitive answers come forward things begin to break down. Quickly, spiraling out of control. A middle age Asian woman yells at her coworker about how she should worry about herself and not concern herself with everyone else's business, especially not hers. The woman turns her back quickly to the shocked woman. Then she pushes a heavy set woman out of her way as, she grabs the telephone receiver placing it to her ear. She then pushes her large 14 karat gold hoop earrings off to the side. She then begins her phone call.

As, the commotion intensifies within the data processioning office as well as in other offices throughout the St. Louis University Hospital Complex, over the PA loudspeaker system comes the voice of the director of SLU hospital to deliver a message of peace and calm and also to steer the ship down the right path.

"Attention all St. Louis University Hospital employees and patients. This is Hospital Director, Bill Hopkins. We have received information from the Mayor of St. Louis as well as from the Chief of Police regarding a band of attackers, who have victimized well in excess of 90 people. Highway 44 has been shutdown in both the east and west bound lanes. The Chief of Police has also recommended for those already at safe place to stay there for now, 'till the situation is under control. The entire hospital thanks you for your calmness and patience during this rather unpleasant time for all of us. Thank you."

The message ends for those who are not in the emergency room area. For the doctors and employees inside the E.R., Hospital Director Hopkins prepares his troops for the influx of new arrivals that will soon be flooding into SLU's E.R.

Back on the eighth floor the data processors have began to heed Mr. Hopkins message and calm themselves. Claretha Philips walks over to the office window and looks out at the sky, on this early autumn afternoon. She sees Grand Boulevard and this is a road she has seen for most of her fifty years. Along with the visuals of several fires, which rising high into the air. Her eyes bring in, her ears pick up on the distinct sound of police, fire, and ambulance sirens. Being on the eight floor and sheltered by two inch thick glass. The sound of the sirens still manages to easily penetrate the windows. Once the sounds do not cease, they begin to take their toll on Claretha nerves. Still along with everyone else, she does not yet know the severity of the situation.

Yet, today Grand Boulevard looks totally different than the one she witnessed just six hours ago when she arrived at work planning for more of the same life. Full of the same monogamous thing, day after day, week after week, year after year. This is the way of life in which, Claretha had to accept at eighteen years of age when her oldest of her three sons, Larry, was born.

Being an unskilled and undereducated *'black'* woman in 1976, meant that Claretha had to work hard labor intensive jobs for even longer hours in order to earn enough money for her and the first of her three sons. In the early years of Larry's life this income was supplemented by his father, Bernard's salary as a bricklayer's assistant. This was 'till 1986, when, at the age of thirty five, decided that it was time for a change of life and left his wife of nine years and abandoned their three children for a much younger woman. That even to this very day, Claretha won't admit even exists.

Once Bernard left the household, the amount of money he supplied to support his family became less and less as, the years went by. The support dried up completely in the recession era of George Bush Sr. in the early 1990's. She adapted to these new realities and decided to attend St. Louis Community College at Forest Park. After five and a half years she earned her A.A. degree in Computer Technology.

It was with this newly found knowledge, she was able to gain the leverage that enabled her to leave her humbling job of cleaning the offices and bathrooms of this very hospital. To now being the manager of the Data Processing department and ten other employees.

Now faced with this situation, Claretha tries to calm the women in the office.

"Everyone heard now what's going on from Mr. Hopkins, let's all just give a call to our loved-ones and get all that good stuff buttoned up. Then we'll get back down to work again."

She delivers the message in a confident, but friendly and informal manner. It's a shame that she, herself isn't as confident as the strong woman that she projects to her employees. She just can't get this horrible sinking feeling out of her gut. The feeling that one or all of her kids are in some kind of real danger. She knows Larry, her oldest, is capable enough to take care of himself. Her middle son, Damien is shady enough to make sure he'll keeps himself out of harms way. But, it's her youngest son, Victor which has her most worried. He is only seventeen years old and right now he is working at Food World grocery store on Jefferson Avenue and LaFayette.

He is able to be working at this time of day due to his high school's on the job training class. Claretha has always been extremely protective regarding him and now with this outbreak, as they are calling it on the radio, her instincts tell her that something just isn't right. But, what is she going to do? The phone-line has been busy at Food World, probably that Puerto Rican girl that works there, which Claretha doesn't like. She's always pushing her workload onto somebody else. She's not going to lose her cool and calmly walks over to her desk and gets back to work logging in number after number. Yet, her thoughts are focused on the second rate food store on Jefferson Avenue.

12

12:18 P.M. OCTOBER 28, 2006

Victor is walking around the empty and deserted parking lot of his employer's for the last nine months. Before, his eyes he is witnessing the beginning of something that will devastate St. Louis, in a way which no one could have ever thought possible. He sees people fleeing quickly from the streets. Then, his attention focuses on the police driving down Jefferson Avenue. They stop any car or pedestrian they come across. The police are out in force projecting their level of control over the populace. Just in case anyone thinks that this situation might become a perfect time to loot. Stealing anything they might want.

The side streets of Allen and Russell, are witnessing young African American youths grouping together, seeking to figure what is happening to the people of their community. The groups enlarges as more and more dissatisfied boys join in. The agitators within the groups stir anger fueling the fear within the other members. The scene quickly spirals out of control.

And with no enemy in sight to confront and with the cops not on the scene, the mob goes about tormenting their own neighbors. Like the vortex of a hurricane, car windows are smashed. Nothing of is taken just broken into without care for ownership. The residents of this area are helpless to confront a swirl of sixty whipped up youths. They retreat back into their homes, now they must deal with not only this outbreak, but also several mini riots. Frantic, repeated calls to the police go unanswered as, the circuit's are overloaded.

As, the group enlarges forcing it's way onto Jefferson Avenue. This is then the disenfranchised mob are confronted by an aggressive police presence. The police number only twenty, but have the advantage of being organized and disciplined. The mob on the other hand, which is being fueled by rage and frustration. The closer to the police the group gets, the more spread out it becomes. As, it tries to avoid direct confrontation with the hard baton's the cops carry. As, some men challenge the police most of the teens run scattering back to the safety of their homes or hangouts. For those unfortunate to challenge the police officers, they are learning the hard way the consequences for their actions. Stick after thunderous stick is slammed across the bodies. The statement the cops delivers, shows their mentality now during the outbreak.

Then on the artery of streets the police spread with the sound truck as well as the squad cars announcing that there is a curfew in effect and the citizens of this neighborhood need to stay in their homes and not leave until further notice. Law enforcement announces that the residents this area should not try to leave where they are via automobile. The roads are not passable in all areas. This is by order of the St. Louis Metropolitan Police Department.

Victor stands in the parking lot in awe at the events happening all around him, then a cool fall wind blows in from the northwest whipping at him. He, quickly zips up his pullover jacket turns around and walks back towards the empty supermarket. As, he steps through the automated doors, he dreads going inside and takes a moment for one last gaze around.

The dark blue sky above him, the sound of birds singing in the trees across the street and then the contrasting presence of the police vehicles, one of the cities three police helicopters above, and finally the distant cries of the retreating mob. Victor turns around and walks into the store not knowing how long this ordeal will last and hoping that whatever has happened will be over A.S.A.P.

He starts to walk over towards the service desk where, the manager of the store is located. Zoran Dudakovic is there with one of his many nieces that he has hired within the last two months. He is desperately trying to get through to his wife, who is at the couple's home in Crestwood which is located about thirteen miles southwest from Downtown St. Louis. The call being placed is now his fourth attempt within the last ten minutes. The previous three calls have been dropped because of the overloaded local telephone circuit's. In frustration the mid-forties Bosnian man slams the phone down against the base. The phone dangles by it's curled cord 'till finally the angered man grabs it in haste and guides it back to it's home. Victor sees his managers disposition and approaches the service desk with caution as, he already has felt the managers quick tempter. As a result he's learnt whenever possible to give him a wide berth.

"Did you hear what the police said out there? They said you can't leave were you are now!" Victor starts another sentence but is interrupted by his manager.

"Yeah, I know." He says matter of fact to Victor. "The radio has been blaring it for that last ten minutes now." He gives a pause in his speech.

"But I guess it took you that long to bring in those six or seven carts, huh?"

"Well, what should I do now, then?" Victor asks knowing he'll get yelled at for instinctually not knowing what he should do next.

"I don't know, why don't you keep yourself busy breaking those boxes down out back."

The manager says in a *'I'm too busy and can't be bothered to deal with you'* style. With that he turns around and walks to the rear of the store. Past the vegetables and fruit then by the baked goods, as he finally passes the meat department. It's then that he arrives out back of the store with just him, the boxes and the trash.

Box after box, he slashes with his box cutter as, he then throws them into the recycling dumpster. Victor grabs a hold of about ten cut boxes and tosses them over the side of the dumpster. It's then that, he hears a banging noise on the chain link fence that surrounds the three garbage dumpsters Food World has stored out back. He jumps easily over a couple of flattened boxes to see what it is. When Victor first looks at the three men banging on the fence, he assumes they are normal for this area of town, homeless people. Thinking they are looking for either some money or free food. Just, thirty minutes ago they were those very same homeless men. Now, though they are nothing but non-human living dead creatures!

Victor yells over to them.

"Hey, what the hell do ya want?"

He tries to project a *'don't mess with me'* attitude. Hoping instead not to show the vulnerable person, he feels in this erie situation. He receives no reply from the three at all. It's then that he notices that a huge chunk of flesh has been ripped from the early sixties, shaggy looking black man's neck. The creature stands still trying desperately to draw air from the gapping wound.

Quickly, turning and looking at the other two creatures he notices that one has it's entire left arm ripped off at the elbow. As, the tendons and ligaments dangle. The third creature standing outside, has no flesh left in it's thigh until you reach the femur bone. The creature missing it's left arm, runs straight ahead smashing hard into the fence. The fence gives way moving, backwards two feet then the creature is sent flying backwards as, it falls on it's backside.

The creature is resilient though and is back up his feet like a Slinky. Then along with the two other creatures, they all three charge the fence. Victor hears the over stressed metal links begin to give way, he knows it's only a matter of time before they break through. Feeling the threat of these three unholy aberrations. Quickly, he leaps over the boxes and in the excitement misjudges an old spaghetti sauce box landing hard on his left shoulder. Against the brick wall of the supermarket. But, he's not wasting time on thoughts of a scrapped-up shoulder. To hell with that shoulder, he thinks.

Victor flat-out opens the metal door, jumping inside the market, as quickly as possible he, slams the door behind him with force. As, soon as his hands touch the lock, it's locked. With all the noise being made from his actions, Bill Monte, who is the head butcher of Food World leaves his meat slicer to see what could be happening at the back door.

"What the hell you doin', Victor?"

"Tell everyone somethin' crazy is happen' out here! There are some really fucked up bums tryin' to get in here. One's missing his throat and he's still comin!"

Victor panics and runs over to Bill, who is completely shocked by what he's just been told by the teen.

"What!? That can't be true."

"The hell it isn't, they're right outside that door tryin' to get their asses in here!" He yells at Bill, as he has to defend himself.

"Well, I am going to see what's going on out there!"

Bill tells him as, he walks away from him. Victor is floored that Bill doesn't believe what he just told him.

"No! Don't do that!"

Victor says in a panic, but Bill doesn't follow his advice. Maybe the reason is because his rank in the employees file is low and Bill believes that he knows more than Victor does.

Whatever the reason, Bill unlocks the final sliding bolt swinging the heavy metal door open. Finding the three homeless men exactly as, Victor described just moments ago. He stands in the door frame taking in the images, his brain does not seem to grasp a hold of the situation. Directly, to his right is the older black ghoul with that disgusting bite, from which it's throat was totally ripped from it's body. Without warning the creature jumps from behind the Waste Management recycling dumpster. Some, how the creature managed to make it's way over the seven-foot high fence which protected Victor, so well from the creature's attack first strike.

The creatures are not the most agile of being's, it comes stumbling unbalanced at Bill, who now gathered behind him are four other employee's. Including Victor, the store manager and his niece, Alma looking on to see if *'it'* is for real or not. Unfortunately, for all of them, what they are witnessing is for real. For others, who have not yet witnessed these walking dead first hand, the news reports are real, as well. For something that started one hour ago on Highway 44 at the Kingshighway exit, which at the time seemed like just another car accident, which happens all over the United States thousands of times a day.

For reasons yet unknown, the cargo that Michael's van was carrying unleashed a new virus upon the world. Which, the population was in no way prepared to handle.

"Slam the door!"

Victor yells to Bill as, if he is the only one capable enough to command him to do so. The creature is coming closer and closer to him. It moves with a big swivel at it's hips, as if they pivoted on jelly instead of muscles and bones. Underneath the fence slides one of the other homeless creature's, this is the one missing much of it's thigh tissue. This one can balance it's self much better than it's companion. Quickly, coming towards Bill and the others located behind him. The creature moves towards it's target. Unexpectedly, the creature bumps into it's partner that is missing it's throat and both creatures fall clumsily to the ground. Knocking the creature against the dumpster and it slouches down before it regains it's balance. Finally, getting back to it's wobbly base.

"Do it now, damn it!"

The Bosnian manager yells at Bill, who finally snaps out of his state of shock and slams the metal door locking the half inch thick sliding bolt lock.

"What the hell is going on with them? They're all torn up missing body parts and everything. How is that possible?"

Bill says stream of conscious to himself, which happens to be heard by the other members of the group.

At that moment, Victor is the only member of the group with the good sense to think of the other way that the creatures can easily get inside the supermarket.

"Hey somebody needs to lock the automatic doors at the front of the store before those things get in that way."

It is then that everyone realizes just how vulnerable they really are. That now a different kind of thinking will be needed in the future. That is if you intend to survive for long against this ever growing number of living dead, which are mounting in St. Louis.

The manager screams at Alma Poljarveic, who is the manager's wife sisters oldest daughter, also a Bosnian. Who settled in St. Louis in 1999 along with most of the rest of the Bosnian Muslims fleeing the ethnic cleansing of Slobodan Milosevic's Serb regime.

"Alma, you need to disable the doors, now!"

"Zoran, I don't know how to disable the doors."

Alma's thick Balkan accent makes her reply almost impossible for the non-Bosnians to understand what was said.

"Damn it!"

Mr. Dudakovic, shouts as, he begins to run as quick as possible to the front of the store. He's just past the meat department and midway down aisle four. Now he's at the end of the aisle and has a full view of the front of the market. Zoran, spots the three homeless creatures meandering towards the automatic doors which still remain operational. In a haste the manager jumps over the turn style that blocks a lane from being used, when there is not a cashier to attend to it.

Outside the supermarket, two newly rejuvenated members of the living dead walk unsteady from the parking. These two comprise of a forty year old woman and her eight-year-old son. Both are making their way towards the entrance. The mother and son join with the other three creatures. When Alma sees the shape of the three appear, she screams and frantically yells to her uncle to hurry up before the creatures can get in the store. The manager reaches the automatic door and pulls his keys from his pocket. Quickly, putting the key into the slot and turning the lock. He locks the doors shut, as the three creatures are only three feet away. The mother and son are a further five feet behind them. The creatures continue to march towards the automatic doors trying to gain entry to their victims, even though the door is now locked. The creature with it's throat missing walks straight into the door.

"BAMM!"

The creature slams it's self off of the shatterproof glass door. The force of the impact throws the creature down to the black grooved magnetic sensor pad for the doors. The fallen creature's two companion's come towards the door. Drawn to not to the door, but to the people inside. For the creatures, it's like a moth and how they are attracted to those insect zapping devices that used to rid people of the insect's annoying behavior.

The two standing creatures stop for a brief second beside their fallen comrade, as if something inside of them still remembers the qualities that make each one of us human. Feelings and emotions such as love, attachment and compassion. It is these qualities, which we associate as being distinct human qualities. We see them as different than other living things, which we share this world with.

These creatures which rise up from death seem to share at least some of our qualities, but on a very primal level. The two creatures are now joined up by the mother and son. Together they leave the fallen creature behind, who is still trying to regain it's vertical base. When the creatures reach the locked automatic door they scratch and smack at the shatterproof glass. The glass vibrates from their repeated thumps, but it does not show any signs at all of giving way for now. From across the glass blood is smeared in long streaks, as the creatures are desperate to gain entrance. Now everyone inside of the independent grocery store has made their way from where, they once where just a minute ago. The entrance is crowed as everyone wants to see exactly what is going on outside. Besides the eleven employees of Food World, there are fourteen customers which creates a horde just past the empty checkout lanes. Confusion is beginning to set in among both the customers and the employees as well. The chaos is realization that there is no way out of this store right now.

Translation: They're all trapped inside! From out of a crowd a heavyset black woman who name is Janis, yells out.

"Let me the fuck up out of here!"

Her statement is echoed by a few within the crowd, but many of them see this locked store as their only protection. It's a good place to be for the time being. For now, atleast.

The store manager, Mr. Dudakovic speaks up.

"Look everyone, the radio and the police said that there is some kind of mass violence happening all over the city right now. We are best to stay here."

Even before his last syllable is muttered, Janis yells to everyone again.

"Well, hell the police and the radio said it so damn, it must be true."

Her same supporters, yell again backing her statement up. As, the overwhelmed and under supported Bosnian manager begins his rebuttal, a white man dressed in a business suit with his leather briefcase at his side, tells the group his story.

"Look everyone, I just came off of 44 in both directions it's total gridlock. Fortunately, I was near the Jefferson exit, so I took it. The radio reported over twenty have been killed at the Kingshighway exit and even more have been killed at the Kingshighway and Manchester intersection. The news reports said that the victims were partially eaten."

The businessman's tone gets more direct towards the group members.

"And looking at those five out there, it seems that this has spread over to this area of the city, now."

With that statement, he stops speaking and everyone in the groups curiosity is perked up.

"Well, what did they say is behind this?" Asks a woman in her forties, while clutching at her black leather purse for extra emotional support. "I just wanna be able to get to my kid's school."

"Like the manager tried to say a minute ago, it seems to be some kind of mass violence, like a riot of some kind." The suit says.

The black woman, Janis again raises some concerns of hers.

"What kind of riots, do the people eat each other? And how are those things out there still walkin', I mean look at that one's neck and then the others leg! They ain't got neither one of those body parts. Why aren't they fallin' down dead?"

She gains more support behind her on those sets of unanswerable questions.

"I don't know why but, I do know it's much safer in here than out there with those things." Says the manager.

13

12:25 P.M. OCTOBER 28, 2006

LOCATION: Chouteau Avenue and Jefferson Avenue

Sitting in the passenger seat of his St. Louis County government Chevrolet Suburban is Ellis Bishop. Known to everyone except for his mother as just *'Bishop'*. He has been with the City and County of St. Louis for the past twenty five years. His roles turing that time might have changed many times during the proceeding twenty five years. But, the one thing which has remained constant is the fact that when something goes wrong, every mayor of the city has called upon Bishop to come up with a solution. He sits uncomfortable in the passenger seat assessing the damage to the city.

Balancing on the dashboard of the suv, is a laptop computer that is constantly being updated via the wireless LAN. The data streaming into the computer consists of everything that government officials have available to them. From which areas of the city that have fallen to the creatures, to the estimates of the numbers of the creatures which are swarming the city. Then finally computer models which show the areas the creatures might invade next. Also, much to Bishop's dismay is his mobile phone that continuously rings. Seeking from him to know, what if anything can be done to prevent the spread of the creatures outbreak.

UNINFECTED POPULATIONS IN ST. LOUIS CITY- BREAKDOWN OF INFECTION RATES:

Areas of infection-	Percentage of uninfected
Downtown	5%
Midtown	15%
Soulard	8%
Dog Town	13%
South City	16%
Central West End	11%

The eighth time in the last three minutes his mobile phone rings.

"Yeah!" Bishop barks.

We can not hear what the other side of the conversation is saying to him, but you can hear that he is agitated at the caller.

"No, I told you already Rick, who is the head of the Alderman of St. Louis. There's no fuckin' way to prevent the Downtown from being ran sacked. You'll have those damm things will be marching up the Arch in a hour!"

And with that last statement he throws his Nokia phone down onto the tan carpeted floor board. Bishop turns to the driver of the suv, Jones his partner who has remained quiet through all of this and is merely taking everything in.

"They still don't grasp things at all do they?" Jones asking rhetorically.

"They never fuckin' will either. They're just too Goddamn stupid, that's why!"

14

12:31 P.M. OCTOBER 28, 2006

Located Downtown St. Louis is Washington Avenue one of the area's main streets, the center of attraction, which provides the backbone for this recently rehabilitated central business district. This area of town in the past was the headquarters of numerous Fortune 500 business along with the countless side business that opened to serve the influx of workers. Ranging from sandwich counters to dry cleaners and other shoppes. They existed in order to service those, who had the means.

This period of time existed prior to the early sixties, when the phenomenon known as white flight began in earnest. People who used to live in beautiful turn of the century two-story homes, left them behind in favor of new subdivision homes complete with cul-de-sacs and swimming pools. But, it was much more than simply white people fleeing the perceived threat from the black community and other minority groups. The affluent class did not want '*such people*' living next door.

So, you had the beginning of the '*new*' America, reinventing itself economically from a leading manufacturing country to now a service-based economy. This created major problems for Northern manufacturing cities of Cleveland, Detroit, Pittsburgh and of course St. Louis. Factories closed by the thousands in these cities and in this area of St. Louis businesses were hit extremely hard hit. For this was the garment district for shoes, hats and leather products.

The location of these businesses were contracted out to countries with cheap labor like China, Malaysia and Indonesia. Eventually, Downtown St. Louis was left with hundreds of large buildings and factories with no one to occupy them. The building and factories were too big to ignore and due to asbestos were to expensive to justify tearing them down. It was not till the mid-1990's, when residents urged the politicians, who in turn put the necessary pressure on the developers (with the promise of free properties and generous tax credit's) to get interested in the city (mainly the Downtown/Riverfront area) again. The scaffolding went up and two years later a once dormant shoe factory became home to thirty two loft apartments that appeal to the Bohemian type of person.

It's ideal for the individual that doesn't mind paying $850 a month and dealing with all that metropolitan city living has to offer. Including traffic and street noise to the homeless people, that hassle you for your spare change at many of the restaurants and bars. The Downtown Commission even has posters displaying information, how patrons can handle and avoid these unsavory characters.

Inside one of those very loft apartment buildings on the seventh floor in apartment 7H, is home to a thirty three year old environmental lawyer and part-time artist, who never really sells any of his art work. Yet, he continues putting on his art shows anyway. Lance Wagner lives with his girlfriend of the last three years, Leah Thompson. Leah is twenty seven years old and works in the St. Louis Galleria at the Express store. The relationship between the two of them, to say the very least is rocky. On outward appearances everything seems to be great with the couple, but Leah's close friends would tell you a different story. On more than one occasion, Lance lost his self-control physically assaulting her, on numerous occasions. But, he's no dummy, he always punches her in the chest, stomach and back, where curious people would not see the bruises on her body.

On the day that the outbreak hits St. Louis, Lance and Leah are both at home in their loft. There is an impatient knock at the door, on the other side it's their friend Chris from the loft below. Lance, who is in the middle of his latest project, an abstract painting of Leah's naked body, which has a emphasis on the vagina. He yells for Leah, who is balancing the budget for the household, to get rid of whoever it is at the door.

She looks through the peephole and instantly recognizes Chris and opens the door. She starts to welcome him in her usual friendly voice even though she knows Lance wants her to get rid of him A.S.A.P. But, she doesn't get the chance to do so as he launches into a near hysterical speech.

"Aren't you guys freaked? I can't believe it! Everything is going fuckin' crazy and you two are acting like nothing is happening."

Chris stops for a second and looks around. Hearing all this, Lance comes over to the door to see what's going on. She interrupts him before, he can start up again.

"Chris, what are you talking about?"

Leah has learned to be calm in dealing with *'artistic'* people as they tend to over react to things on occasion. Before he can respond, Lance gives him a big, phony.

"Hey, how you doing?"

Chris doesn't respond to the question of formalities and politeness and instead responds directly to Leah's question.

"It's all over the radio, TV, everything." Chris says very quickly.

Lance asks him, what he is talking about.

"You don't know?" He asks sounding shocked as a person could be.

Both of them respond the same way. "What?"

He takes a moment doubting even himself. "**THE DEAD ARE WALKING!**"

Leah and Lance look at each other.

"Very, funny stuff asshole, what the hells the matter with you? Why are you wasting my time with these silly ass jokes?"

Lance asks Chris, as he walks back toward his canvas.

"I'm not joking at all, turn the TV on then! We're getting the hell out of here 'till it's over."

With that, he turns and hurries towards the stairway. Taking two, three steps at a time. Quickly, he's out of sight. Disappearing into a sea of panicked voices down below.

"I'll see what that jerk is talking about!"

Lance says as he picks up his DirecTV remote control and turns on the television. Lance hit's the guide button and selects KEJK News Channel 5, the local national affiliate. What pops onto his screen amazes him. There, from a helicopter's vantage point, he along with Leah witnesses the horrors that are occurring just two miles from his loft on Highway 44. Chris was right is the very first thought, he has. The second is how in the world is this possible. The third is what kind of danger 'am I in? Lance yells for Leah to come over to see the TV.

"What is it?" She asks him.

"You won't believe this! Chris was right!"

She has a look of disbelief on her face which turns to sheer terror as she sees the *'impossible'*—the living dead walking.

"What?!" How can this be?"

Leah asks Lance, who is just as dumbfounded as she is about what's going on.

"Does anyone know what is happening?"

Her voice starts to become more panicked, as she receives no information on what could be behind this horrific event. There is the information bar running at the bottom of the television screen alerting viewers that, a state of emergency has been called by the Mayor of St. Louis. Until the authorities have the situation of the walking dead under control. Also stated at this time there is no solid proof as to how or why the recently dead are now beginning to walk. The recommendation of government officials is to remain where you are as long as, the location is secure enough.

They both watch as the city and life they once knew is beginning to fade away from memory. Instead, it's being replaced by this new and distorted picture of a populace under attack from an enemy which we could of never could planned for. The creatures only reason to exist is to destroy everyone within their sight.

"What should we do, Lance?"

She asks him, as she still wait's for a reply to any of her many questions. Lance takes a second to digest everything.

"I don't see any reason to get all hysterical, Leah. I mean think about it for a second, 44 is over three miles away and why would they come down Washington Avenue anyway? To pick up some art? Don't panic, we're fine."

He tells her and fells pretty good for calming her down, too.

"But, Chris said..."

She tries to say but is interrupted by Lance who already has the answer

"Cause, Chris is an idiot that's why."

She believes what Lance tells her and walks away from him and towards their bedroom. Flopping herself down on the king side bed, she tries to forget about what she just witnessed on the TV. If, only Leah would have walked over to her huge bay windows instead, looking out. She would've noticed the panic and chaos on the streets happening on 5th Street and Olive Street. Which is only a quarter of a mile from their front door.

15

12:43 P.M. OCTOBER 28, 2006

The time is 12:43 pm and people are working and doing business Downtown. The streets are crowed with cars, while pedestrians navigate through the traffic and down the sidewalks. It's a mixture of white collar types along with their counter parts the average office worker in a more casual dress. Mixed among them are adolescent African American males hanging out in smaller groups, of only four to five as not to draw to much attention from the police. It appears as, if no one has heard the announcements by the authorities or they are simply not putting much stock in what they said.

They should have headed the warnings. From the alleyway behind the YMCA on Locust Street, an overwhelming series of strange wails followed instantly by groans. Everyone within ear shot of the noise is startled and put on guard. A professional woman in her early thirties, who looks like she works at one of the many financial banking institutions located in this area. The obviously spooked woman looks all around yet sees nothing but tall building enveloping around her. The groans now become more startling, as they grow louder and more intense.

The level is comparable to living next to Lambert St. Louis Airport, hearing one of it's Boeing 747 taxing for take off. When the people in the vicinity of 5th and Locust finally are exposed to what is behind the noise, there's no way possible any of us, who were not there could comprehend the sheer terror they felt in the last troubled moments of their lives.

"Oh, my God!!!" Is shouted by a woman.

As, the horde of the living dead finally emerge from the darkened alleyway with it's broken and jagged asphalt causing the maundering dead to trip and stumble as they arrive on Locust. Without warning the creatures begin to brutally and viciously attack their victims. Sparing no one they come across.

The first victims to succumb, are a small group of young college students who are about to enter the YMCA for a work out. The four guys are caught completely off guard and fall quickly. The creatures grab hold of them and rip into their flesh. Then deeper into the toned strong muscle. It's an especially brutal attack. One of the victims is a five year old little girl, who's father, was routinely dropping off his child at the center's day care.

Just like the others, no mercy is shown or given to anyone including the young and helpless. The terrified toddler is separated from her father, while trying to run anywhere other than here. It's then when a, girl that is dressed like she is thirteen, but is really in her early twenties grabs the screaming toddler by the arm. Attempting to bring the child to her to mouth to tear a huge gash from her body, but the child fights against the young creature. They both go flying into the horde of at least thirty deranged creatures.

As, soon as the tiny child hit's the horde, she is sucked into the center of the vortex and is gone forever. The defenseless and dumbfounded people, who were on their way to whatever task, run for whatever cover they can find. Some people are frozen in fear and they die a quick but gruesome death. For them they, no longer know what it is like to be stalked, hunted and finally eaten alive by the pursuing creatures. The only hope after being attacked is to be so physically destroyed that you cannot possibly come back as one of those *'things'*. The creatures only seem to really want to destroy the people who fight back hard against them. It's as if they know the only way to increase the species number is to keep their victims, somewhat intact.

The panic and fear of this uncontrollable horde creates is intense. The creatures chase after you into any buildings, you might try and duck into. They smash through your car window to prey upon you. Their relentless quest to destroy is unparalleled. For these able to get ahead of the horde and run down Olive Street it soon becomes an even greater nightmare. As, a man in his fifties is turn apart as, a Chevy Suburban traveling out of control down Locust, which results in disastrous accident. A second car tries to swerve but ends up smashing head on with a delivery truck carrying office supplies. The accident is a disaster in two ways, first the people who are dying in the nine car accident. Second, more importantly is the fact Locust is totally blocked off by the wreckage. This has now shut down both lanes going east or west.

After only moments, traffic is backed up a quarter mile. If the people inside those vehicles only knew the horrors which are coming their way. But maybe it's better for the people inside to have these few minutes of innocence. Before the carnage begins upon them. The creatures movements are decisive and blindingly quick as they pounce on the terrified motorists. Without advanced notice, the creatures smash through their automobile glass. Their arms already damaged from being turned into these things. Even though their bodies show the signs of damage, no blood drips from their extensive wounds.

One such victim is a elderly woman diving a tiny white Hyundai is trapped inside her car by the seat belt. Two creatures crash through the hatchback window, the second creature ends up in the old woman's lap. The impact of being hit by the ravenous creature stuns the woman. The ghoul pulls in a deep enraged breath before, it raises it's head, quickly biting into the throat of the old woman. The elderly woman shouts in terror, but it's of no use. Where their was once loose wrinkled skin there is now a throat completely ripped out. Blood splatters across the front windshield. The old woman attempts to exhale one of her final breaths, but is unable to do so.

The second creature in the rear cargo hatch feeds on the ripped out throat of the old woman from behind. With the devastating wounds, the elderly lady slumps forward and her forehead smashes against the steering wheel. Causing her horn to blare in the crisp, fall air mixing with the rest of the chaotic sounds.

Within five minutes the horde stormed in totally, destroying an entire four block area of a major city. Turning it into a wasteland created in the image of themselves. Cars smolder from colliding with each other. Bodies and their appendages liter the scenery. Blood has soaked the roadway and sidewalks. Trash blows in the western wind with no real purpose. In all this the authorities, with all of their abilities to control man made problems such as riots and fires are of absolutely no use in this situation.

Their presence is no where in sight. Maybe their numbers are too few to be stretched out this thinly. Or, maybe they know the true extent of this catastrophe and know what little abilities they have left would be of little use. Plus, add into the equation that no one has heard of any survivors after being affected by the steadily, growing number of creatures.

So, for the residents living in the fire zone, they are now officially and completely on their own. On the street nothing moves, there are no sounds, life is total devoid here. The creatures have now moved onto other areas, where more victims lie ahead.

16

12:45 P.M. OCTOBER 28, 2006

Back up at apartment 7H, the telephone starts ringing and Leah reaches over to the night stand picking up the cordless phone and pressing the talk button on.

"Hello?"

She asks wishing no one was there so she could hang the telephone up and get back to starring at her ceiling. Forgetting everything out there. But, the person on the other end of the phone line launches into a panicked conversation.

"Leah, dear what's going on? I clicked my computer on and there on my home page, it says that travel to and from St. Louis has been suspended!"

Leah knows from that very first syllable uttered that it is her Mother!

"It's nothing mom, just some junk happening all the way over on Kingshighway. It's really nothing."

"I don't believe you Leah! There's been 60,000 killed already and the Downtown is surrounded!"

It's with that statement that she knows that absolutely nothing will ever be the same again in her life again.

"The entire Downtown?"

She asks interrupting her mother speaking.

"Yes, and they say the police are unable to stop those things. What are you going to do Leah?"

"I gotta go mom, I love you."

With that Leah's mother's line goes dead, the dread of not knowing if she'll ever see or speak to her daughter begins to overcome her. Leah throws the phone against the wall, it lands on the concrete floor. She yells for Lance.

"Lance, your fuckin' wrong their all around us now! We're trapped!"

Saying this she knows full well, it might get her punched, but damn it sooner or later you gotta make a stand. This is Leah's stand right now.

"What are you talking about?"

Acting if he could really care less and he really couldn't.

"Those damn things aren't just over on 44, there all around us now! We could of got out of here in time, if you weren't so fuckin' pig headed!"

Then BAMM!

With that statement, he does what comes natural for a guy like him and smacks her right across the mouth. Leah falls to one knee, blood begins to form on her upper lip. She looks up at him in complete disgust.

"Want to run that smart mouth again? You stupid bitch!"

"We're fuckin finished anyway, so hit me again you fuck!"

She commands of him.

"How do you know so much?"

"Check the news. The entire downtown is surrounded, 60,000 people have been killed, there's no cops left or anything. We're finished."

Leah is tired of his stupidly. Directly in front of their loft apartment on Washington Avenue people are abandoning their vehicle where ever they happen to be. A Dodge truck is left on the sidewalk outside of the now vacated Tangerine Restaurant. A second is blocking the intersection at Washington and Tucker. If you look closely, you might catch a fleeting glimpse of a live human being.

It seems that people now are learning that being caught in the open with these creatures is not the smartest thing to do if you value self-preservation. For the creatures hunting us humans, the emphasis now has now went from a pure free for all. To now a game of hide and seek to get to their human victims.

"Just look outside!"

She says to him, as she looks out on Washington Avenue through their huge bay windows. He walks from in front of the television set, which continues to play a loop of the same footage that they have been showing through out this whole ordeal.

"No way?"

Lance says to nobody in particular. He knows that now, he is in trouble. Thoughts and plans start to run through his mind. Getting into his mid-size pickup is a no go after seeing the condition of Washington. Even, if he could get off of Washington, the other roads are littered with abandoned vehicles too. Then God only knows how many of those damn things are out around the streets. Patrolling no, the truck is no good and if, the truck is out, you can throw out trying to escape by foot, as well.

Think, think, is what runs through his brain. But, nothing is coming and then there's that little problem of Leah.

"I'll keep her with me 'till she becomes a liability to me."

"That can't be too long, huh?" Lance thinks. What can I do to get the hell out of the city? Nothing coming to mind.

But, there is! He thinks, he has the perfect idea.

"I got it. That dude in 4B has that motorcycle, what is it? A.A.A. Ducati Monster. That cool-ass one that, I have wanted to ride for a year now. If it's still there, I take it!" Lance says to himself.

That's the *'big'* idea that he has.

"I got it, Leah!"

He says finally with some kind of plan.

"What?" She asks with hardly even paying attention to whatever he has to say.

"That motorcycle in the underground lot!" This is Lance's epiphany.

"Will it work?" She asks getting more interested now.

"You got anything else?" And with that his plan is put into full effect.

17

12:48 P.M. OCTOBER 28, 2006

Officers Darryl and Barton are approaching the southern edge of Kingshighway. The entrance ramp to Highway 44 is now a quarter mile away and within their sight. As the two drive farther south, the scene is getting worse and worse as they slowly make their way through the wrecked and smoldering vehicles. Which now litter and block almost the entire roadway.

"24 to Base." A moment passes.

"24 to Base, come in! Over!" For a second time in less than ten seconds there is dead air in between Barton and dispatch.

Darryl has to finesse the squad car around a over turned Dodge van which is blocking the middle of both lanes. The front end of the squad car passes by with no problem, but the rear quarter panel scrapes against the bumper of the van. The rear tire runs over the detached front bumper, and the squad car's rear end rises high into the air in response.

"No, reply from dispatch?" Darryl asks, never diverting his attention away from the road.

"You forget how to drive there?"

Barton gives Darryl a hard time, but he isn't paying any attention to his partner's humor. Instead he is paying more attention to the worsening conditions that are right here in front of him.

"What do you think? Why isn't dispatch going through?"

Darryl asks Barton, as he scans the surrounding vicinity.

"Don't know, maybe it's some kind of area wide violence. But, nothing has been brewing around here lately."

He says to Darryl. From out of nowhere something catches Barton's eye. A black woman runs right out in front of their squad car. Barton yells at Darryl.

"Watch it!"

He slams on the brakes. The tires smoke, as they try to gain traction on the debris-covered road.

"Where did she come from!"

Darryl yells out. As, the squad car comes to a stop. They both jump out of the vehicle. Looking around to where the woman should be. Yet, there is nobody.

"Where the hell did she go?"

Barton asks his partner, as two more figures appear. They run across the rear of the car. Out of the extreme left of Barton's eye, he catches their movements. Instantly, he in one quick motion grabs his gun and spins around to see the two figures running around the rear of the car. The creatures make wide circular movements. The figures now begin to come around the front of their squad car. When Darryl spots that Barton has drawn his gun, he does as well. He knows that Barton is a bit of a hot head, but he wouldn't pull his gun if he didn't have a good reason.

They both now see the situation before them. To their south is sixteen of these creatures slowly making their way towards them. To their west along Northrop Avenue are seven badly mutilated one's, who are not moving towards them at all. But, instead are feeding on the remains of the occupants in their car. Behind, to the north lies a littered, yet safe escape away from this ever growing threat. Then before the two can react, to their east comes a humming noise comprising of groans which, as the seconds pass becomes louder and louder. The hordes of new creatures have mauled their way from Highway 44 in every direction conceivable and now come towards Darryl and Barton. The hums now a mere ten seconds later have grown into an unbearable, inhuman roar.

When Darryl and Barton finally see the horde, the sheer number and horrible appearance of them, is almost a sight that the two police officers cannot believe is truly for real. Well, over 200 pop-out to shock the men. But, these creatures are unfortunately very real. They are the remains of us that due to some produced virus have reanimated from death and now seek to destroy us, to ensure their own survival. The creatures movement towards Barton and Darryl is by no means maundering, they are coming at them at a full run.

The sound from the hundreds of footsteps marching down the asphalt is like a marching army battalion. It seems that the creatures retain a lot of their human intelligence. They have set the two in a perfect trap. The creatures have strategically, hit their target's, all the way to Manchester. Then pull themselves back to regroup, wait for the virus to take hold and add to their already impressive numbers. Now, this time their prey has come to them. It's as, if the creatures are playing a masterful game of chess. They attack then wait, their numbers increase. As, well as luring their prey even deeper into their territory.

Darryl yells to Barton.

"What now?"

He looks around at the situation. Barton doesn't answer his long time partner and instead fires his pistol. The crowd of creatures are roughly hundred and fifty feet away. One bullet, two, three and then four, he fires into them. Nothing happens. Not one of them drops. The only effect it has, is it knocks them back a step or two, before they continue forward once again.

"Fire at them, damn it!"

Barton barks at his partner, in response he fires at the ones closest to his south.

Bullets number one, two, and three are expelled from the chamber. Bullets one and two, smack deep into the flesh of a white woman. Who before it's death was a nurse, you can tell by her outfit. Yet, the bullets have absolutely no effect on her. Bullet number three is aimed higher, by mistake, and hit's the woman in the upper forehead. The bullet splatters brain matter from the brain cavity, all over her dirty blonde hair. But, the only difference is this time, she drops down to the ground and does not get back up.

"Hit them in their damn head!"

Barton does as his partner says. Shot five misses and hit's into a black man in it's late forties. Shot number six is right on. Even at hundred twenty five feet, the powerful 9 mm handgun split's the man's skull like a shattered melon. Darryl discharges his remaining bullets and two more creatures fall. Barton is forced to reload as, well firing off more shots before Darryl screams over the deafening noise.

"We can't keep this up much longer, there's too many of them. We need back-up!"

Darryl knows back up is not coming. They're either dead or plain won't come into this situation. He knows they're on their own.

"Let's get out of here, it's too hot!"

Barton says this knowing that even with 100% accuracy their six-round clips are no match for the relentless number of creatures lining up against them.

"All right, we'll back up to Manchester and regroup there, ok?"

Darryl says as then they both run back to the squad car.

It's then that Barton hears the old man thumping against the metal cage that everything clicks in his mind.

"That old son-of-a-bitch is one of them, Darryl!"

The feeling of carrying a creature in his squad car is too much for him.

"I'm gonna shoot that fuckin' thing!"

He sees Barton's anger. As, well as his temper, it begins to over ride his common sense.

"We ain't got time for that now, we gotta leave right now!"

It takes him a second to process that Darryl is correct. He agrees and they both jump into the squad car. The high-performance V-8 engine roars over the cries of the creatures. Quickly, they begin to swarm around the vehicle and block it off. Darryl does not sit around waiting for this to happen. He slams the transmission into reverse and floors the gas. Instantly, the rear tires burn out and he quickly whips the steering wheel around forcing the vehicle to spin out in a complete 360-degree turn. The front end with it's thick push bumper slams into the side of the Chevy Express van. Reacting, Darryl reverses the vehicle getting it pointed ahead where the coast is clear. The creatures don't relent, catching up to the rear of the car. This is when several jump onto the trunk.

On his trunk are two creatures which pound on the sheet metal hoping to get their way through. Their goal, getting in the car to get hold of it's human occupants. Now the squad car is surrounded at it's rear and sides with these ravenous things. Fist after fist slams against the body of the car. The noise inside the cabin is compounded by the creature, in the back which kicks, punches and bites at anything that it can. Trying to get free and into where they both are. The creature moans loudly from the pain of hunger which powers them to walk again. It must feed upon the humans. No one knows, yet how long they can exist. Do they need a constant supply of flesh? What happens when the supply runs out? These questions might be answered one day, but Barton and Darryl are lacking in time at the present.

"Get the hell out of here now!"

Barton screams as the creatures grow even more ravenous. Banging on anything they can get a hold of. After a momentary delay, Darryl hit's the gas and their off. The creatures outside continue to bang on the squad car. They don't stop even when they no longer hit the vehicle. Darryl is forced to weave the car from left and right, the job was difficult enough to do when traveling at low speeds. Now through this mine field of smashed and broken down automobiles. There is a Explorer and a Cadillac in a head on collision that, blocks the road up ahead.

Darryl is forced to get as close to the retaining wall as possible to avoid the wreck, but also must not hit the wall. That would put both him and the squad car out of commission. With the two creatures still beating on his rear window, he maneuvers the hulking two-ton machine through an opening of roadway. With less than six inches to spare, Darryl is traveling at more than fifty miles per hour. The front of the vehicle gets through perfectly, unfortunately, Darryl is forced to slam into the retaining wall or rip into the interior of the Cadillac. The squad car bounces off the concrete wall and slams intensely into the Cadillac. The two officers plus the arrested creature are tossed around inside the squad car. The two creatures hanging on the trunk are whipped off. Falling hard against the wrecked automobiles.

The creature which is missing a hamburger size chunk of it's face around the cheek area, is thrown on the hood of a 1970 Buick. It's back is obviously broken, still the creature continues to fight. They will not quit, no matter what is done to them until it seems that the brain is damaged beyond function. With destroying the brain, the creature's seamlessly are indestructible. But, unfortunately this time it's body as let it down. The creature worms and wiggles yet is unable to rise from hood of the Buick. The second creature meanwhile is in better shape with only having bite marks along it's right bicep. Including, a two-inch chunk of bicep muscle missing. That was, prior to being knocked off the trunk and sent flying through the air. Smashing it's way into the Cadillac.

The impact rips through the damaged arm. From below the shoulder as, well as also snapping the neck of the creature. The cracking of the creature's vertebrae separates the brain from the central nervous system. Destroying the creature. It now lies motionless, like the dead are supposed to. Though Darryl is shock-up, and most of the car's metal is torn into shreds from the impact of colliding with both the concrete retaining wall and the exterior of the Cadillac.

The squad car is still in good shape. Most important, it's still running. Even though the left rear tire is blown, the run flat tires that all law enforcement cars are equipped with make's it still useable.

"Is, it still able to make it?"

Barton asks Darryl as, he attempts to steer the ship as straight as he possibly can. Considering the handling of the vehicle is pretty much shot to hell.

"Yeah, it will make it, it's not too bad."

Darryl says with his usual dry sense of humor. He even manages to crack a quick smile to his partner. Barton smiles for a second, then reality hit's him again.

"What's next?"

He asks Darryl even though, he knows that neither Darryl, or anyone else knows what's next.

18

12:53 P.M. OCTOBER 28, 2006

A St. Louis County Police helicopter hovers above Union Station. Down below all that roams amongst the many shops and restaurants, is the maundering dead. Outside of Union Station on Market Street, the creatures roam with not a single human insight. An elderly creature in it's aqua blue nightgown slowly creeps down, Market directly in front of Ray's Original Pizza. Three ten year-old creatures suddenly bump into the elderly ghoul knocking it down to the ground. The creature struggles to regain it's footing and moans in anger. The second before it falls down against a steel railing flipping over and crashes to the sidewalk below.

High above, the helicopter's back end lifts up and it leaves the area. The copilot speaks over the helicopter's in-flight communication system. It's Jones, he turns around to Bishop, who is in the rear.

"Their numbers are greater than thought. It seems the entire Downtown area and along with the Highway 44 corridor has been swallowed whole. For now, the outbreak has not spread past these zones."

Bishop is wearing dark tinted sunglasses and dressed in a drab olive green button-up shirt and dark brown wool pants.

"Yea, for now."

Bishop says almost as a joking.

"Ok, lets get back to the airport, I've seen what I need to."

He commands to the pilot and in a second Union Station and Downtown becomes a distant place that is just another area of St. Louis that now belongs to them, the living dead.

At the Spirit of St. Louis Airport, the black helicopter lands on the helio pad. Golden brown leaves fly up and scatter over the landing strip. It's not 'till the pilot kills the powerful engines that the leaves and dust stop blowing. It's then that occupants disembark from the Bell helicopter. Bishop is carrying a laptop computer and also a legal notepad.

"Well, lets get on with it."

"What do you think they'll do?" Jones asks, even though in his face he knows the answer before he even asked it.

"What do you think?!" He says, as he turns around and continues to walk towards the conference center setup by the local and state officials.

So, far into this outbreak the federal boys haven't gotten here yet. A group is coming in via Scott Air Force base in Belleville, Illinois. They are expected within the next ninety minutes. But, for now at least they run the show.

In the cramped conference room, which was designed to hold fifteen people, now is filled with thirty men as their secretaries run through paperwork. They are busy looking up at television monitors, which display the peril state St. Louis is in right now. The two men walk into the conference room, as soon as they walk through the door frame the Mayor of the City, yells for the two.

"So what's the word?" He asks with great curiosity.

Bishop delivers the not so positive news.

"Not good. Downtown is gone and it's now beginning to advanced to the South as well as North St. Louis. Anything along 44 is gone. Our best bet is to fortify the areas along Highway 40 and 270, to form a complete circle blocking off the West City and county area from these highly infected zones."

"Do you agree with that statement, Jones?" The Mayor asks

"Completely. There is no way to save the Downtown, we need to get ahead of this plan on blocking off the west side, from the eventual infected persons that will come, if we don't do something."

Jones says to not only the Mayor, but also the other members here that can actually make real decisions.

"My only question for the committee here is, can we build any kind of barrier quickly enough to stop them before the infected creatures spread to these areas?"

The Mayor says to the group, hoping to hear the reply he wants and not the answer he knows he will hear. A burly man with a thick brown beard sits up from his blue padded office chair and begins to speak.

"With the amount of equipment, so deep into those infected areas, we will find it difficult to be able to erect any kind of barrier across Highway 40 and 270. The other areas through the city will be next to impossible in less than three weeks."

The man says and then sits back down.

The Mayor jumps to his feet.

"Three weeks?!" We can't wait that long, can we Bishop?"

The senior official from the helicopter steps forward.

"No. I'd give it maybe three days before they will be at our doorstep."

The statement by Bishop sets the entire audience into an uproar. They explode into decisions about what to do, what's next, etc. One man stands up and shouts.

"That's unacceptable! The West County should be sealed within two days and no more!"

The man is Wilson Mead the Alderman of the West County area, his only care is to protect this upscale area from the invading creatures.

The burly guy stands back up.

"That's what it would take to build it properly."

With that statement once again everyone launches into mini debates about what the best course of action is. After a few moments, the Mayor speaks up.

"Let's stop all this bull shit and get 40 and 270 sealed up first. Most of the creatures seem to travel by the easiest means possible. That means the roads. Then we can go from there."

Everyone seems to agree that at a minimum the highways need to be sealed off.

"Bishop, can you arrange all of this for me?"

The Mayor asks Bishop who is drinking a cup of lukewarm coffee out of a styrofoam cup. He looks out the window at this strange, dangerous, new world. Bishop turns back around for a second then goes back to staring out the window again.

"All right, Jones let's get on this one. Get Bruce Roberts from City Works and figure out what kind of equipment he has available. Also we need to get enough skilled and able workers to work on the barriers and fence."

Bishop tells Jones who is already starting to doubt the ability to perform this amount and level of work.

19

1:02 P.M. OCTOBER 28, 2006

It's beginning to rain again. The sky is dark, the clouds of the fast moving thunderstorms are, so black the sun is entirely blocked out of view. The appearance this gives is eerie. Everything appears strange and out of place. High in the sky, sparrows call to others, as they search for food. While, back on the ground crickets chirp, as the darkness has confused the insect in thinking it's nighttime.

The cold rain is being blown by strong easterly winds. Hitting down upon Constance's head, as she looks around the outside of her Benton Park home. Two houses down at the Sullivan's they are throwing the last of their last bags inside of their car. The first thing, she picks up on are how fast and hurried they are.

She can tell that this isn't just some spur of the moment trip. In fact, as they hurry from behind the rear of their garage to the waiting vehicle. She notices that the Sullivan's, who are now driving away have left the front door of their house completely wide open. Why would they do something like that, she asks herself? Then when the wind abruptly changes direction, it begins to soak Constance. Finally giving up trying to figure out what the Sullivan's are doing. She decides to seek dryer ground back inside of her grandmother's home.

"Grandma, you wouldn't believe what the Sullivan's just did."

She says, as she begins to dry herself off with a towel from the kitchen.

"What is that dear?"

Joan asks her granddaughter with some curiosity, as she is quite the neighborhood gossip hound. There's not a piece of gossip that goes by Benton Park, that Joan Bennett does not hear or spread.

"The Sullivan's just threw some stuff in their car and they couldn't get out of here quick enough. They even left their front door wide open. Can you believe that?"

Constance asks as thunder and lightening crashes outside. The brilliant white streaks illuminate the dark exterior an instant before a crashing lightening bolt shakes the foundation of Joan's 105-year-old home.

"Are you for sure? No one would do that."

She asks her granddaughter knowing that something is really wrong but, she doesn't quite know, what it is exactly.

"Yeah, Grandma I was standing right outside when they did it."

She tells her Grandma as if she's crazy or something.

"Why, don't you turn the television on and see how things are progressing on 44."

With that Constance walks out of the bathroom and into the living room. Reaching down she and turns the power button on. The picture pops on the screen. At first, she doesn't know what to make of what she sees. The screen is filled with images of people being ripped apart by these crazed deformed creatures. They destroy all that they come across.

On Highway 44, is footage of fleeing motorists being hunted down and slaughtered. A heavy set black woman is caught trying to exit her mini-van. Two creatures pounce tearing, the throat of the woman out. A chunk of her flesh the size of a pork chop is pulled from her body. The resulting loss of flesh forces the body to pump blood by the quart. The woman falls to the roadway, the two creatures do not stay around long before they seek out their next victim.

The next image she witnesses is a group of seven creatures attacking a family of three. The young girl of the family, falls behind and is the first to be attacked by the group. Her mother turns around screaming for her.

"Vicky!"

But, it's in vain, the child screams in pain as, a skinny and greasy white creature in it's early twenties tears into her forearm. It's the first thing that the hungry creature comes across. Teeth smash into flesh as blood flows from the multiple bite wounds. The young girl screams as, it continues to attack. Then the creature goes right for the girls struggling neck and clamps it's mouth hard on the neck. That's when the blood begins to flow, quickly down on her shoulders. Finally, rolling down her tiny back. The child's eyes close and are never to open again as a human. When those once innocent eyes reopen, she will be one of them. Transformed into, a creature. Constance turns her head away from the television and yells for her grandmother to come and see what is happening.

Startled by her tone, she quickly enters the living room and rests her hands upon the young woman's shoulders.

"Look at what this has become!" She insists to her grandmother.

Joan watches for just moments before the knowledge of self-preservation kicks in.

"Get your brother on the phone, get him back here. I'll lock the doors and pack some things, just in case."

Constance is on the phone and finds out that Nick is on Magnolia, right by Tower Grove Park. He informs his sister that traffic is insane. Blocked up no matter what side street you try. The last statement that, he makes before his mobile phone fades out is that he is going to ditch the car. Walking the remainder from Magnolia back to their home. Constance reluctantly hangs up the telephone. She then informs, her worried grandmother of Nick's plans.

"I hope he'll be okay."

She says to Constance and to Nick as well.

20

1:13 P.M. OCTOBER 18, 2006

In the span of thirty minutes the number of creatures flocking to the outside of the supermarket, has swelled from the five to now in excess of eighty. The creatures continue to pound away on the shatterproof glass, they are desperate to get inside. The terrified people inside hold their breath with every punch that resonates through the fifty feet long section of the front window. It shakes and sway's with every energetic fist, which smashes into the glass. But the window holds. For, how long can it hold against the mob of creatures which continues to multiply by the minute?

That is the thought that is on everyone's mind right now, but no one is talking about it. Or, what might be the cause of this plague.

"How, long can we stay here?"

Victor asks the group as, he jumps down from the checkout counter. The other members of the group don't pay any attention to his question. He's alone here thus is not connected with other the members. His social status is quite low in the group. He must accept to be a follower within this group or face what life might be like on his own. No, he isn't going to do anything like that. He'll do what is needed of him cause, it's much better being safe then being a leader out on your own.

"We gotta figure out exactly, how bad the situation is out there."

The man in the business suit says to the manager.

The manger snaps back at him.

"Take a look out our front window, that will tell you everything you need to know!"

He angrily points towards the hoard just fifteen feet away. Four of the group members break away from the meeting, tired of the constant arguing by the various individuals, who force their views upon the other group members. The moment, the manager sees the four people walks away, he yells to them in his thick accent.

"Hey, where do you think you're going?"

The four men and women look around at each other, as if to decide who should be the leader and speak for the remaining three members. Finally, a white woman with long black hair speaks up.

"We're getting tired of everyone yelling at each other. Nothing is being achieved!"

The remaining members look at each other, as if the fault lies with one of them. These twenty strangers have been forced into a situation with no real guide to resolve this unbelievable situation. In, only thirty minutes the dynamics within the group has changed from being a situation of relief to a group arguing about this and that. As, well as which member of the group is right and which is wrong. Their efforts to try and make sense of what's happening to them have been halted due to their own inability to sympathize with one another.

"No one has even bothered to talk about how we should stop those damn things from getting inside of here. No, let's talk instead who should be the leader!"

The statement to the group was given with the hope that maybe the group will come together with some idea to prevent the creatures from simply smashing through the window. Devouring everyone inside if they do. The manager asks if anyone has an idea. The raven-haired woman says to everyone.

"What about duct tape to hold the glass in place longer?"

The businessman jumps into action and mentions that the tape would not hold anything back from coming through the windows. He goes onto to say what they need to put up is boards over the windows. It's then that Janis yells at him.

"Hey, what you think you're in? Home Depot or somethin'?"

She is so proud of her comment, she starts laughing with the other two people in her circle.

The group begins to drift back into chaos when Victor speaks again.

"What about movin' the shelves over from the aisles to front of the windows. Load 'em up with junk where they ain't goin' to tip over."

The thought was so simple and easy, but the adults had not come up with anything nearly, as simple and effective as the one he just suggested. Everyone begins looking at one another. Then agrees that yes, this idea is definitely the way to go.

The businessman asks that the group start unloading the shelves directly in front of the store. Moving them towards the front windows of the supermarket. Everyone has a task with a mission and begins to unload the can goods, bottles and boxes of dry goods.

The aisles quickly begin to become over crowded with the remnants of the shelves. It isn't long before the first shelf is emptied and four of the men hoist the awkwardly long aluminum shelf up in the air and towards the crowd of hungrily awaiting creatures. It's then as the shelf is put into place that two women along with three teenage girls, start to fill the shelves. First with heavy bags of sugar, flour and rice.

With all of this commotion taking place in the front of the windows, the creatures are being whipped into a crazed fever. With greater intensity the creatures pound and smack against the windows, as their numbers continue to escalate. Howling and moaning in their desperation to enter. In the distant background of the city, the people inside the supermarket can hear the faint sirens of the few remaining police cars. Then at the front of the store, a black creature with blood coating it's hands continues to pound, hard on the glass.

The creature continues, as the blood is smeared on the glass. The blood is then smudged by other creatures as they try to break in. But, the glass is holding and up until this point has not budged. The people inside are organizing in case the creatures, do break the window. Five minutes into it, the windows are now half blocked out with the aluminum shelves. Loaded down with many heavy objects, it would be quite difficult to push the shelves over from the outside. As, each and every person goes about their task, everything is going as well as can be expected under these trying circumstances. Everyone is cooperating and working well together, with the common goal of stopping the creatures from getting inside and killing everyone of them.

21

1:22 P.M. OCTOBER 28, 2006

Conformable in the knowledge that he is indeed correct, Lance tells Leah the finer details of what, his escape plan are.

"We're headin' out of this apartment. Those things be all will over us and eventually they'll get, in here."

Leah takes one last look around the apartment for a second. She views all the things in life that up till this time have defined who and what she is. All the possessions that brought her joy. She is now forced to leave them behind. Will she ever get to return to her apartment? What exactly lies out there, in this new and frightening world?

She, is about to get a crash course in the new ways of life. As, soon as they exit the door of their peaceful apartment immediately they are exposed to the outbreak. Both now wish they could escape reality and instead be in someone else's life. Anywhere right now would be safer than the hot zone of St. Louis. Even the most dangerous areas in the world like Iraq, Afghanistan, or Sudan, never have experienced the horrors which are being committed here, right now.

The residents that remain of the Art Loft apartments are trying as well to escape. It's a scene of desperation and confusion as over sixty people, try in vain to escape from the apartment building's main staircase. The fleeing residents are caught like a lobster in it's trap. The reason being at the entrance to the complex, there is a group of ten creatures barreling up the staircase in hungry pursuit. Drawn to the panicking residents, by the sound of their screams and cries for help. The staircase for the Art Loft's is a standard spiral design. Unknown to the fleeing residents is the drum of noise coming from the approaching creatures.

Moving in the opposite direction of the creatures are a band of frenzied people. The creatures make their way quickly up, the staircase, moaning and whaling in anticipation of the fast approaching feeding opportunity. The tile lined staircase quickly becomes wrapped in the frightening noises. Yet, for those focused on fleeing their attention is elsewhere. The crowd hurries. People are screaming at each other in a desperate panic as they clog up. As, they round the tight wrought iron railing of the staircase.

As, the residents finally reach level three. This is the exact moment in time that the residents of the Art Loft apartments on Washington Avenue, have the unfortunate displeasure of meeting up with the lead pack of creatures. The crazed creatures waste no time, as the terrified people attempt to retreat. Desperate to make their escape from their attackers. But, they fail to do so. The reason the staircase is banked at such a steep angle that it is packed beyond capacity. As, more and more residents continue, desperate to escape.

"Oh, my GOD!!"

Is the first sound made by a scruffy looking white male in his early thirties. Seconds after he utters the statement, that was indeed his last. The terror stricken man is attacked by two creatures. They lay siege upon the man. Violently, flesh is torn by the creatures ravenous teeth. The besieged man falls to ground. The two creatures go down with the man as well. Unable to abandon their prime feeding opportunity, the man lays there with blood continuing to pour from his body. Making a very slick obstacle in the tight staircase for the fleeing residents.

Once they take their fill of the man's flesh, the creatures join their compatriots to attack further. The horrified residents at the back of the pack turn around to see their worst nightmares, an approaching army of the creatures chasing for them. For those unlucky to be trapped in the hallway, death is delivered in a quick and certain fashion. But, for those unfortunate to simply be bitten by the creatures managing to escape further damage.

A long painful transformation from human to creature has began in their bloodstream's. Because once injected into the human blood system, the yet unknown virus which the creatures spread is introduced into our system. Systematically, it begins destroying and mutating our DNA. The virus then goes about altering the framework of the genes to resemble their own.

No, one yet knows how the virus achieves either the rejuvenation of cells or how in fact the virus alters the human DNA from a simple bite wound. Perhaps one day a scientist will discover the answers to these questions and school children everywhere will study the findings. Learning about this process in their science classes. To those which remain after the creatures outbreak this will just be a bad memory from long ago. But, right now reality looks bleak.

Standing anxiously by their metal door, hearing the horrible screams emitting from the hallway. Lance quickly pulls Leah away from the door and back into the center of the apartment.

"We aren't goin' out there now! No, fuckin' way!"

He says to Leah, but more so to himself. Then he hurries over to the bay window. His eyes soak in the events before him. Tired of witnessing person after person chased down in front of his eyes and slaughtered. Lance turns back around and faces Leah.

"We'll have to wait here for the time being atleast. I don't hear anyone making it out the staircase or even out on the streets. It's safe inside of here as long as those things don't, know we are in here. Then once we don't hear them that's when we know it will be safe to get the hell out."

As, Lance finishes up his statement, Leah thinks to herself if they will escape the confines of St. Louis or she is destined to end up like the countless others who have disappeared from this outbreak from the creatures vicious attacks?

Forty-five minutes have elapsed, Lance braves himself for one quick peak outside the apartment door. Not a sound has occurred outside the door for over thirty minutes now. Yet, still Lance has not had the bravery to open the door just yet. His nerves are tethering on a razor's edge. He knows, he has do something, pacing for the floor the last forty five minutes hasn't done the trick. No, he knows he has to open that door. And that time is right now.

The door cracks open a inch, the rays of the afternoon sunshine streak through the miniscule space. From behind the door appears the first trace of who is there. The bridge of Lance's nose begins to peak out, as he scopes the scene to whether it is safe enough to flee the apartment or not. Immediately, his eyes take in the horror which happened to so many of the residents. They were unfortunate enough to be caught in the staircase with no way to escape the creatures rampage. Atleast now there is no movement that he can detect. But, he's not going to take any unnecessary chances and proceeds away from the door with extreme caution. Behind him, Leah begins to follow closely behind him.

"Get the hell back in there."

Lance yells to her under his breath, as not to draw any unwanted attention to himself. By any creatures which could still be lurking around the apartment complex. To Lance the last thing, he needs right now is Leah sneaking up behind him when there still could be those creatures lurking around. He has now ventured out ten feet from the apartment. The tension is running high through his body, as he snakes his way down the hallway exploring just what's out there. He still figures that if he does see those *"things"* he can still safely get back to the apartment.

But, what then? They would now know that he is inside, it would then be just a matter of time before they broke in. Lance knows this, but this is his only option left. He must somehow find a way to escape not only this building but even more importantly this city

All is still and quiet the further down the hallway, he walks towards the staircase. Carefully, he navigates over the trash strewn hallway. The fleeing and panicked residents left behind everything they once considered valuable. Down below his right foot is the remains of the resident of apartment 4C. Besides her, broken German cuckoo clock and other personnel effects. Dropped then tramped over by the furious footsteps of the departing occupants just forty five minutes ago. Also a remnant from the creature attacks are the pools of blood which have collected in the spots were the sloped hallway begins to form more of a bowl shape pattern. Along with the tile floor being coated in spots. There is also numerous smears of blood down the walls of the hallway. As, well as much of the staircase, too. Still, Lance tries his best not to focus in on these sights, he has to keep his attention, to what lies ahead of him.

Inside her apartment, Leah wonders wildly about what has happen to Lance as he's been gone now for over twenty minutes. What has happened to him? Has he been killed by the creatures? Has he been forced to hide from them? Or did he simply leave her to fend all for herself? All of those questions could easily end in yes. Yet, she wait's patiently for him to make an appearance. It must be due to her being beat down by him so much. That's the only reason, most of her friends can figure out, why she stays with him.

After thirty minutes have elapsed since Lance left, she is now certain that he's is not coming.

"What to do?"

Is the thought that singularly runs through her mind. The question finds no answer, and she is back where she started. Stuck. Deep inside she knows she must do something. She just can't hang out at her loft and hope that this outbreak will some how pass her quietly by. No, it won't and she understands the situation she's in, but which path should she choose? Pick the wrong one and your destroyed by the creatures, as they rip you apart. Then within minutes you rise and become one of them.

BOOM! The front door of the apartment slams shut. Leah who is scanning the streets below for some reassuring sights from her bedroom window. She isn't seeing any out there. Endless lines of the maundering living dead roaming the Downtown streets of St. Louis. But, the sound of the door snaps her out of her daydream nightmare and into reality. She bolts through the door way and finds Lance standing there. He appears there annoyed that she is not waiting right there for him.

"Why, the fuck wasn't the door locked?"

Leah looks around, the love she was feeling for him is gone. Deep inside, she now wishes that he would have been killed by those creatures.

"What an asshole."

Is her thought, as he walks toward her.

"Are you going to answer me?!"

"Cause, so you could get back inside if those things were chasing you. That's why."

"Well, I didn't find anything. Nobody is left. The things are gone and so are the people. The only way anyone would know something happened here is all the blood that's left behind. I don't know where they are, those things must have carried them away or something."

"So, what do we do now?"

"We're getting the hell out of here! I have the keys to that bike already." Lance dangles the keys to the Ducati in his hand and has a cheerful look on his face. A look that says. 'I know more than you do and I relish in it.'

Down below, in the subterranean parking structure all is empty. All is also silent except for a few drops of rain water which seep in from the outside. The water falls slowly into a shallow pool, which is collecting in the corner along the support column. Then the distant sound of foot steps. Soon the sound becomes compounded by the acoustics of the parking structure. The anonymous footsteps soon have a voice, as the sounds begin to envelope around the parking garage. Echoing between the ceiling, floor and then the walls. The sounds of the voices are faint though and inaudible. The footsteps soon develop into a wall of sound around the abandoned parking garage. For the for the first time the voices become understandable.

"Are you sure we'll be able to get out of here? The whole Downtown is a mess,"

Leah says to his back, as she plays catch up with him.

"Don't worry this little thing will get us where ever we need to get."

He moves even farther ahead of her towards the bike. He finds the bike sitting alone away from the vehicles. The doors are left car open, the remains of items left behind from a population forced to flee from their lives with absolutely, no time to prepare. Let alone ponder what they should take with them or what should be left behind.

Lance sits on the powerful V-twin bike and inserts the key into the ignition. Asking,. Leah

"You ready?"

She doesn't say anything to him instead, she straddles herself over the rear seat of the motorcycle. When he feels her body get closer to his back, he lets off a small crocked smile, that says.

"Yeah, I own you and don't you ever forget that bitch, or you'll get one of these."

As, a mental image of his fist pops into his mind.

"All right, let's get the hell out of here!"

He shouts to her before he starts up the engine and twists the throttle on the handlebars. The engine growls to life and resonates with thunderous echoes through the enclosed garage. Before, she fully tightens her arms around his midsection, he launches off in first gear. The tachometer springs from idle to over 4000 rpm in less than three seconds.

The wide rear tire spins on the damp surface then shoots off a rooster tail of spray high into the air. Leah momentarily loses her balance and almost falls off the bike. The sound of the exhaust is deafening, as they launch through the parking area. There is nothing but lifelessness among the abandoned cars and trucks. Lance speeds his way through the parking area without regard for what happened to those vehicles owners. He simply doesn't look at them.

Obviously, he has no regard for his fellow man. He broke in to obtain the keys for the motorcycle. Not knowing whatever or not Billy was inside or not. More importantly, he did not care. He was getting those keys one way or another. Lets just say he was motivated to do '*whatever*' was needed in order to get those keys.

The motorcycle roars up the exit ramp. Leaning the motorcycle into the bend as the ramp begins to snake around a 360-degree bend. You can hear from the exhaust note when he backs off the throttle. He gets in the tight left-hander a little too hard causing the tires to bark from a lack of grip. Adrenaline begins pouring through his body, he knows he's in over his head with riding a motorcycle. The motorcycle sways towards the wall. Metal from the frame scrapes against the concrete wall.

Sparks fly, but quickly Lance regains control of the bike. He manages to pull it off the wall and back into the center of the road. Leah grabs hold even tighter fearing for her life due to his recklessness. He throttles the bike back down and starts making his way up the ramp again. Exiting, to the outside on Locust Avenue, which is one block north of Washington Avenue. The scene is here on Locust is the same one on Washington.

Cars, trucks and buses are left abandoned wherever they stopped. Bodies litter the road and sidewalks. Those that do not roam, have been so badly destroyed by their attackers that the body parts are unidentifiable, other than being just pieces of flesh. No, longer are they recognizable as Mr. Johnson or Mrs. Peterson. They are now merely destroyed flesh in much the same way the creatures did when they attacked the living only hours before. The same silence in the subterranean parking garage exist here, on the street. The only sound that brakes free of the powerful grip of silence over St. Louis, is the light rain that has been falling intermediately for the last twenty five minutes.

The birds swoop from the air, feeding upon the flesh of the fallen. It is not yet, known known what, if any effects this virus might have on the wildlife. The only remaining thing on the street is now the creatures. It's walks along with no specific place or purpose to it's movement. The noisy motorcycle powers onto Locust Avenue, from the beginning of things Lance is forced to deal with difficult obstacles. Directly, in the center of the road a van was smashed by a full-size pickup, splitting the side of the van's metal cargo area. The results are four-dozen boxes filled with the documents of patients medical history spilled across the road. Containing everything from a birth last July to a blood test result yesterday. The boxes continue to spill thousands of pieces of information all over Locust. The rain continues to fall weighing the soggy papers down even more. Lance is able to weave the front end of the motorcycle in between boxes which are piled five deep.

The engine continues to roar with it's deep throaty growl.

VROOM! VROOM!

The sound is echoed back and forth in between the brick buildings on the opposite sides of Locust. Still the two have not attracted any noticeable interest from the few creatures which are struggling to make their way around the street. A black creature with a large size chunk of flesh missing from it's neck and shoulder is on the prowl. On the sidewalk the creature finds a meal. The remains of a human, it reaches down and ravages the loose thigh muscle of a woman. The rotting foul mouth of the creature is full with the rigor mortis induced flesh of the thigh.

He carefully maneuvers his way through the obstacles. The creature is standing one hundred feet to the north. He points the front wheel north and is on a collision course with the huge creature. Starting out on the sidewalk quickly up through the gears. First gear, provides for the quick acceleration needed. Second, makes the five hundred pound bike fly down Locust at forty five. It's when, he hit's third gear and sixty mph that the huge creatures sits up from it's macabre meal for the first time.

Lance notices the terrifying figure and is forced to abandoned the sidewalk, taking to the littered street. Instead, a three-car pileup threatens their path. He takes evasive action, as the Ducati swings towards the center lane, Leah grabs hold of him even tighter. Swinging in between the wreckage of a mini van and suv. The gap between the wreckage is no more than two feet, not to mention the gas and oil which coats the ground. He approaches the gap, brakes and down shifts down a gear into second. The rear of the bike hops, as there is too much speed for the gear to accept smoothly.

Lance looses control of the bike for a second as the bike wiggles, four feet from where he'll enter the gap. Where there is a good chance of both being killed. Even worse yet, they could be badly injured from the accident. Then the creature, which is a mere thirty feet away eats one of them, as the other is forced to lie there unable to defend themselves. Then after the creature is done feeding on you, you'll transform into one of them.

With only a foot to spare, he regains control on the machine and enters the narrow gap. Lance manages to execute the timing and distance perfectly. The only snag is some debris in the path that, he needs to drive over in order to finesse his way way through the narrow opening. He figures that running over some bits of the two vehicles metal bodywork is better than the alternative of crashing into the two wrecked vehicles. He does so, the instant before the front tire runs over the bumper of the Dodge Caravan. Lance yells back to Leah.

"Hold on!"

He swings around the rear of the mini van, if he had the time to glance over at the open tailgate. He would have noticed that both the front and rear seats are coated in the former occupants blood which has now seeped itself into every fiber and is as sticky as maple syrup.

But, he's got more pressing issues to deal with right now. He managed to get them both through two of the obstacles. Immediately, he's forced to deal with a third one. The suv cracked it's oil case as a result of the accident. Spilling the fluid over the road. The spare tire was also knocked off the rear. Leaving him only eighteen inches in which to place the bike. Eighteen inches to make it through or wreck. Twisting the gas, the engine responds instantly with more horsepower and torque to the rear wheel. Lance is thinking, that the faster he goes, the better it seems to handle than at slower speeds. You gotta go with what you feel.

'WHAM!'

The bike revs by the suv managing to avoid the oil. Lance is forced to run over the smashed body parts of the vehicle. With the speed he's going, the front-end of the bike is launched a foot in the air.

'SMACK!'

The front tire lands back on the road and with a 'RAAW! The front tire lets out a trail of white smoke. As, he moves his focus from that obstacle, he finds the curb on the north side of Locust Avenue approaching him faster than he would have wished for. Bringing the bike into a power slide. 'WHAM!' As the brakes lock up and stop the tires in only ten feet.

The huge African American creature stands up from it's feast. Walking with slow curiosity to the northwest. With each step, getting closer to the stopped motorcycle which idles noisily just feet from the curb. Leah looks around attempting to gain her bearings. She turns around and gets her first look at the new rulers of St. Louis in person. She lets out a scream from deep within her sternum, screaming loudly.

The sound is echoed back and forth amongst the brick walls of the building's. The curious creature reacts to the vibrations in it's ear drums. The hunger which burns within it's large, empty stomach sends a signal to it's brain that demands it, to replenish the contents of it's stomach. The creature lets out what seems to be some kind of reply to Leah's scream.

"AHHH!"

It continues to make it's way towards them. Even though the massive creature is alone and moving at her slowly, she desperately pleads with Lance to move now!

He looks over and can see that the creature is coming towards them extremely slow. Inside, the sick sadistic head of his, he decides to let her sweat it for just a minute longer. When the creature is eight feet away, he finally decides to make his exit. The 992 cc air-cooled engine roars to life as he accelerates from first gear then second. It's only then he shifts the Italian powerhouse into third gear. Speeding up to forty five mph does, he back off the throttle. Traveling west down Locust, the epicenter of the invasion seems to have missed this particular street with it's destructive force.

There is only a limited amount of destruction here in the form of wrecked automobiles. As a consequence the walking dead are few and far between in this area of Downtown. Lance cruises around a few obstacles that are in his way with no problems. He knows that even though this street seems somewhat safe, the possibility of death increases the longer they cruise around Downtown looking for a way to escape. They need to get out of here fast! So, now he has come to a crossroad. Should he try and get to Interstate 70 to his east and head either to the west or south county? Or possibly try and make it to Highway 40?

The debate rages in Lance's head. He knows that 40 is a hot spot but he doesn't have a clue about what I-70 is like. He wonders to himself. Could the situation there the same as on 40 or by some kind of miracle, could it in fact be the perfect ticket out of this living hell. Their goal a march towards a new life with some semblance of normalcy.

Finally, he comes to a decision while, the motorcycle is stopped on the sidewalk at 20th street. This is as good a place as any to finalize plans. There are no walking dead to be found. They seem to work together and hunt their prey in large groups. This style of hunting has proven extremely effective for the new species, which has been introduced to the previously dominant species, just two hours ago.

Leah leans forward from her barely adequate seating space, asking him what is going on. Scanning the area to figure out what the situation is, Lance can see that everything appears calm at least for the moment.

"We need to go to I-70."

Lance says to her, loud enough to overcome the engine noise.

"Why?"

She asks with her voice barely audible.

"It's our only chance out of here. Every other way will get us killed."

He turns the motorcycle around and heads back east on Locust.

This time around, he goes faster than he did the first time through. The obstacles and many hazards, no longer pose the threat they did the first time. It's when he gets to 14th Street that the monstrous creatures maunders in the middle of Locust Avenue with bright red blood covering it. The body below will not be able to be identified or claim by a member of their family. That is how bad the creatures attacks are. The blood is smeared all around and drips from it's disgusting mouth. The ghoul hears the noise of the motorcycle again, it's head and body goes from a slumped position to an excited, upright one.

The extremely overweight ghoul hurries towards the direction of the motorcycle. The surroundings are completely different than before when they came west just minutes ago. Now there are more of those creatures which have wondered their way from the side streets surrounding Locust. No doubt the creatures are drawn to the area from the noise of the motorcycle's exhaust. On the street, a teenage girl, who is now a creature and still wears her Catholic school uniform. Collides with the huge black ghoul. The tiny-framed creature falls to the ground, moaning.

It's as if it is communicating, it's unhappiness, in a language we do not understand. The black creature doesn't seem to notice and continues west. Lance blows right through the intersection at 15th, the original creature is now joined by ten others. More and more also appear emerging suddenly out from alley ways. As, well as stumbling out from ransacked offices and warehouses.

Lance knows now he's in trouble, if their numbers get much higher. But, for now, he is all right and simply avoids the creatures with ease as they try and approach their intended victims. With the huge creature is in the center of the road, Lance thinks.

"I wish I was driving a Mack truck, I'd run over that fat son-of-a-bitch."

But, he is not, so he's forced to adjust his plans slightly. He leans the bike sharply to the left, the bike immediately jumps to the left. The confused creature reacts slowly and does not know what to think of the sudden and quick movements of the bike. Missing the opportunity for food causes the creature to moan with disappointment and anger. He got through a few creatures, but what lies ahead when and if he and Leah make it to I-70?

22

1:37 P.M. OCTOBER 28, 2006

On the Highway 40 on the Clayton Road/Skinner exit, three Caterpillar 814 F wheel dozers carry concrete guardrails, which are used to block cars from jumping over the overpasses on the highways. But, that's not their use today. They are being placed to block the oncoming horde of creatures which are expect to flood this area within the hour. Moving from the city and inevitably will be wrecking the surrounding county area.

The eastbound lane of 40 has already been finished, now all that remains is for the triple fence to be erected to stop the horde. The scene resembles that of a ant colony. The little worker ants, going about their duties and the foremen supervising all the work. The diesel engine of the bright yellow wheel dozer blows out a series of thick chocking black smoke into the air. The bucket at the front slams down and smashes into the pavement. The guard rail slams hard against the metal of the bucket and breaks off a two foot hole around the edge of the guard rail.

Four workers come over quickly attempting to position the object out of the bucket and onto the highway. They push and pull. Finally, the four men make some progress and the five hundred pound concrete block finally begins to budge. The driver puts the Cat 814 F wheel dozer in reverse and begins to very slowly back up. The wheel dozer emits a ear piercing beep-beep noise to warn anyone who might be careless enough to stand behind the machine as, it is moving backwards. The block slides quickly out of the scoop bucket. Immediately, the workers attach metal braces to the ten other guardrails. They're strapped in three places with the quarter inch metal straps and with that, the westbound lane of 40 is sealed off.

On the overpass at Hampton Avenue, a half of a mile away. Bishop and Jones are standing viewing the scene that is quiet and surreal. A major metropolitan city of 2.5 million and there is not a single car coming in either direction of the highway. Which at this time of day would normally be congested. The entrance and exit ramps are completely swamped with the cars of those who, attempted to flee an unexpected attack from the creatures. They sacked and destroyed the residents of St. Louis quickly and with little effort. The badly damaged bodies of the fallen lie next to their automobiles. The stench from the dead begins to fill the air with an overpowering and overwhelming smell. Bishop and Jones ignore the smell. Instead, their attention is focused on the progress half mile west of the highway.

"I know it's like plugging a dam with your finger and hoping some how it will stop the inevitable from happening. This is what they think will stop them, so it's up to the only ones dumb enough to know better but not smart enough not to get the fuck out of here!"

He turns to the right and looks upon the empty campus of St. Louis Community College Forest Park Campus. The three-story building has walls mainly of glass. The resulting chaos caused the students and staff, who went through during the initial outbreak to panic. Desks, chairs, along with any other items with in arms reach were thrown through windows. Anything had to seem better than being eaten alive by these things. So, with no options left, they jumped. Now the creatures patrol the hallways looking for anybody that might have escaped the first invasion.

"There ain't a fuckin' person left here is there?" Bishop asks rhetorically.

"We better get back to the work area, they look like they're finishing up."

Jones says to Bishop, as they both look down at the highway below. The wheel dozer begins it's journey back on a flat bed semi-trailer and onto it's next assignment. Four men are rolling the chain link fence bundle across 40. Meanwhile two men use post diggers and break through the ground setting in place the fence. Back on the ground, Bishop looks over the diagram of the purposed barrier. He shakes his head in disgust after he views the plans then looks towards the finished project. He grabs his mobile phone and angrily dials. After a few rings, his call is answered.

"How, the hell do you expect this disaster to be contained when the materials I requested aren't here and most importantly aren't coming?"

He berates the person on the other end of the line. If that statement was bad, it gets even worse.

"Well, fuck that! You just sealed the fate for the surrounding county!"

He tosses the phone eight feet into the shrubs along the embankment. Jones comes over to him. He knows the reason why, he is pissing mad right now. At this point he's just trying to calm him down a few degrees.

"That's no way to treat man's most loved invention…"

He says to him, as he's standing face to face with his best friend.

Jones looks at Bishop in the face and delivers in a very serious tone.

"Or most hated as proven by you."

As, much as he wants to hold onto the anger and not let his feelings of disappointment pass, he knows that he should as Jones is a loyal friend. He doesn't deserve the backlash of that government asshole. He gazes down at the highway for a second then raises his head up.

"Yeah, I think I read that. Post Dispatch, right?"

Jones responds with a cocky but friendly attitude.

"Post dispatch? Hell no! The Daily Show on Comedy Central. You know that's my only source for news. You think, they might interview us?"

Both men laugh. Then realize this is the first time they have laughed all day.

"Why don't we wrap this up and go onto our next job."

Bishop half laughing says to Jones. That anger which existed only a minute ago is gone replaced by a feeling of contempt of this new situation. As both men continue to walk past the remaining pieces of construction equipment to be loaded. Two construction workers with two-way radios come running towards them. The two men yells at first are not audible, due to the diesel engines of the wheel dozer as, well as several loud generators. The two workers voices now become audible as they are just four feet from Bishop.

What are they saying, Bishop cannot tell, but from their facial expressions. It's obvious to him it's something is far from ok. A look of total fear and panic runs through the two men. Bishop grabs a hold of one of the workers, he's an older man in his late forties of normal height but on the skinny side. He immediately can feel the man is vibrating like a jackhammer. The look of fear in his blood shot eyes is unmistakable. His partner backs off and allows him talk.

From the scoop bucket of the Caterpillar dozer the concrete divider falls with force down to the highway. The driver panics and slams the dozer into the rear of a city works truck. In a hurry, the workers scurry to avoid the out of control divider. Finally, the extremely heavy block comes to a stop, as it falls on it's side. The workers are helpless as they struggle in vain to pull the block back-up with their bare hands.

The foreman yells to the dozer driver.

"Watch watch the fuck your doin'! Farrell get that dozer down and get that damm divider in place! Hurry it up we got less than five minutes!"

"We just got reports in from the spotters. A whole swarm of those damn things have passed the Grand Boulevard exit and are coming straight down Highway 40. Right, where we are at!"

The man seems somewhat relieved to have gained his composure enough to get the news off of his back. Bishop is shocked at the revelation.

"Did you find out how many?"

Bishop needs to know desperately how many, where these newly erected defensives are not overwhelmed and breached.

"10,000!"

With that mammoth amount, they all know, there's no way in hell that the containment barrier and triple fences will hold back ten thousand crazed creatures.

A thunderous stampede of footsteps roar, as the creatures march with purpose down Highway 40. Packed in between the highway as tightly as possible, not a single more creature could fit in. All ten thousand creatures are driven towards their single common goal, to feed upon and destroy for only source of food......

US!!!!!!

The creatures that march towards Bishop and his men, who are still trying in what seems to many of them to be pointless. These creatures used to be everyday people we all knew. From Bob your neighbor, who is always borrowing the odd egg. To Jessica the cashier at your local supermarket. All the way to Debra your mother. But, these *'things'* as they are being called by the media on the frantic and fleeting telecasts. They are no longer these people. No, your loved one's were killed when they were attacked and transformed into these creatures. The creatures you see have no love in their beating-less hearts for you, any longer.

At a quick pace the creatures stream towards Bishop and the blockade. A ghoul cries out it is soon echoed by all it's surrounding partners. Within mere seconds, the road crew rushing to finish the retaining wall, hears the combined cries and wails of over ten thousand of these creatures. No, man that is busy working here, isn't terrorized by the inhuman and just plain freighting sounds emitted by the creatures.

Without actually being trapped and quickly surrounded by ten thousand of these ultra destructive things. You could never understand the fear which these sixty individuals feel. These men are being stalked and hunted and they know there will be no escape. There where be no way to avoid the approaching creatures horde from destroying them all.

Bishop runs to where his main group of workers are. With his arms waving, he yells for everyone to stop what they are doing. As, the workers spot their boss, one by one they stop working. They've never seen him behave this way and instantly know something is desperately wrong. The roar of the machines is silenced. Bishop has everybody's attention.

"Everyone needs to stop now and get the hell out of the city as quickly as you can!"

His voice begins to break at the end.

"This is finished. There's a army of those things and in about five minutes, they will wipe out this whole entire area!"

He pauses for a second to regain his breath.

"You guys did your best, but you can't stop these things, there's just too many. Now get the hell out of here!"

Jones jumps right in.

"Come on get goin'."

Jones shoos them away with his arms. At that moment the foreman of this operation speaks up

"You heard him, get the fuck out of here!"

When the foreman speaks, they listen. All the equipment which is not already on a trailer and hooked to the trucks is left behind. Pickup trucks, full size tractor-trailers, and the workers own vehicle peel away from the scene. A loud roar fills the air on Highway 40, but it is not from the trucks which just left. The roar is coming from the east and heading towards Bishop and the few remaining workers still there. The roar is that of ten thousand soul less creatures.

They are still well over a mile away but the the sounds coming from them is blood curling to anyone left alive. The empty sounding moans from each creature adds up to make an unholy sound that has even Bishop wishing he was any where but here right now.

As the seconds pass away the impending horde gets closer while the remaining men each say their final goodbyes to each other. Each man knows this will be the final time they'll see each other in this life. Each man displays an upbeat attitude and keep a stiff upper lip. They exchange handshakes to all, then depart to their vehicles. Bishop and Jones take one last final look around the Science Center, Forest Park along with everything else they once knew of St. Louis. It will be gone in minutes when they overcome yet another area of the city.

Bishop and Jones are the last one's to leave. As, they head away, Bishop must be thinking at what a surreal sight is front of him. The highway is empty. The people in this area must of gotten out in time because the only thing on the highway besides an odd car abandoned is them. Bishop is awed by what he sees. As, he rounds a sharp 180-degree curve just past the overpass of Clayton Road. His worst nightmare becomes reality. The highway is completely blocked with vehicles. The creatures frantically chase the few remaining humans still left alive.

The remaining survivors attempt to make their way up an extremely steep embankment. The fleeing residents claw and struggle to make their way up the grassy hill. A hysterical heavyset woman in her late thirties slips and slides backwards down the slippery embankment. Waiting for their prey to fall down to them, five creatures in various forms of damage and decay swarm the overweight woman without delay. The scene quickly becomes a slaughter of a defenseless human. The woman is tossed between a tall black creature and a fat white creature which has a three inch chunk of flesh torn from the shoulder on it's right side.

The terrified woman slips and falls to the ground. This is when the creatures attack with no mercy at all. Flesh is savagely ripped from her body. Two females gather in the feast, more flesh from her forearm is torn down to the bone. The woman screams wildly from the pain as, her blood flows out of the very ragged wounds. The second creature bites through the blouse of the woman and pulls out a tenderloin size chunk of bloody flesh. The two female creatures weaken the woman allowing the three remaining creatures to finish her off.

The creatures pounce on the fallen woman without hesitation. Teeth meet flesh and it's' flesh which looses. A black male creature slips and falls to it's knees. The creature never loses it's grip for a second forcing the woman to the ground. The hungered creature continues to shake and tug at the woman. Skin and muscle tissue can only take so much stress before it reaches it's breaking point.

Pop! A large diameter chunk of flash is ripped from her throat. The creature immediately starts chewing on the raw flesh of the woman. Blood shoots out from the gaping hole, as the heart continues to pump blood to the terrible wound. Sharks sense the properties of blood in the ocean's water. Creatures seem to have the same on the land. The four ravenous creatures descend on the near unconscious woman with each taking turns filling their rotten mouths with their share of the kill. Out of the seven survivors who tried their luck attempting to get up the embankment and reach Clayton Road. Only two reached the top. For the time being they have escaped the fate that the other five encountered.

Bishop looks ahead and that's the moment when, he sees a gang of ten creatures coming directly for him! The creatures are only five feet away before Jones yells to Bishop.

"There's a gap. Take it!"

And with that command, he floors the gas and the rear tires smoke, as they temporarily lose traction. The three-ton suv lunges forward, Bishop has no chance of getting the wide Suburban through with out ramming a parked Explorer, which is blocking the only exit from this scene.

BAMM!

The front of the Chevrolet smashes into the rear of the Ford. With the force the second suv has nowhere to go and smashes into the car in front of it. Glass breaks and metal is smashed, but Bishop now has his room. He wastes no time and begins moving along the breakdown lane. The creatures chase after the suv. Banging and slamming their fist upon the vehicle. Bishop continues to try and get away, but has do so slowly due to the steep angle that truck is trying to overcome. It's an endless parade as one creature after another comes to the vehicle trying to break past the metal exterior and get in the interior.

Within seconds the Suburban is surrounded by creatures, Bishop and Jones know that the creatures will destroy them, if they stick here for too much longer. The only way out of here is up that embankment! Bishop looks over to Jones

"Can we do it?"

And with out hesitation he tells him.

"We have to!"

Bishop cranks the steering wheel to the extreme right. Gunning the powerful 350 cubic inch V-8 again. The huge suv snaps it's rear end, as it desperately tries to catch up to where the front end is now pointed. The steel belted radials dig through the grass and into the dirt and gravel.

Both sides of the suv spit the materials backwards with great force, which pelts the crazed creatures hard all over their bodies. Yet, this minor distraction does nothing to stop the crazed creatures in the rear from continuing to attack. The large vehicle makes it seven feet up the incredibly steep embankment before the Suburban begins to lose it's traction. It now begins just to dig deeper and deeper into the moist dirt of western St. Louis.

Jones yells at Bishop to engage the four wheel drive system. He quickly locks the transfer case into four wheel drive, now with the front wheels pulling, as the 440 pound of torque forces the 3 1/2 ton suv up the embankment. Around their vehicle, there are now over forty-five creatures. Each slam their fist, arms and even bodies against the suv. With the collective force of forty-five, the creatures begin to make the three and a half ton vehicle rock back and forth.

The suv has reached an impasse. The angle it is trying to overcome, is far to great for even this capable vehicle. Instead of trying to force it up an impossible obstacle. Instead, he cranks the wheel to the left, the Suburban quickly goes flying back down the embankment at speeds in excess of forty miles per hour. The creatures who were to close to the steam rolling suv, where either thrown off or dragged down. Bishop notices that they have found themselves up a five foot high retaining wall which is feet away from them now.

The instant that he sees the retaining wall, he slams on the disc brakes and yells out.

"God damn it!"

The brakes lock the tires, but the combination of the steep embankment and it's soft wet earth causes the vehicle to slide uncontrollably down towards the highway below. Bishop and Jones know there is no way to stop. They brace themselves for the impact they both know is just seconds away. On Highway 40, the vehicle with both men is nose first on the highway. The stalled out engine continues to smoke from the crash. Inside the interior all is quite. There is no movement and no sounds inside.

Outside, it's a pure mob scene. Over eighty creatures now have gathered. Pounding and beating on the windows as, well as the body of the suv. Bloody hand prints are smeared across the vehicle. The creatures are desperate to get inside, to feed upon the motionless bodies inside. Bishop's mind is foggy. He is extremely hot and sweating greatly. Also the sense of dizziness overcomes him. His mind is not clear. His eyes do not focus on anything particular at all. He fights through these feelings knowing the last memory, he had was of the Suburban about to crash off of the retaining wall down to the highway below.

Random thoughts then begin to flood his mind.

"Where am I? Did those things get me? Am I one of them? Would I know, if I was one?"

Then scenes from the Lake of the Ozarks. Fishing from the banks. The sound of the water gently breaking along the banks. The smell of the aquatic life, below the water's surface. Then a thought comes to his mind.

"I wanna go back there."

He thinks to himself. And the clear and perfect memory of a time, that as of October 28, 2006 no longer exist. This memory brings Bishop out of that dream world and into this new world. He is immediately forced to witness the relentless creatures doing whatever, it is they can do to gain access. Before, he has time to register these events, a cleaver creature takes a metal rod from a wrecked wagon's luggage rack and smashes the passenger side window of the Suburban.

With the creature's lack of balance and coordination to swing the rod downward, it fails to break the dark tinted window completely. Instead the hit causes a spider web of cracks to form across the window. He knows he's trapped, and it seems he's out of options. A second whack with the rod causes further stress in the already fragile windowpane.

Then four creatures focus in banging and beating 'till the glass breaks in small fractured pieces. Bishop can see their hungry crazed faces, as they ram through the jagged glass. Their bluish skin ripped wide open while no blood comes out. He looks around, outside his driver window are easily sixty of those things!

There's no escape possible in that direction, the creatures have that side blocked off. There's nowhere left to go. Trapped inside this coffin of a suv, he knows his time is now. Yet, how is it possible in a world controlled by a loving God. That anyone would be forced to not only wait for their own death but be eaten alive by these flesh eating creatures. Then to top it all off, you become one of them. This is just one of the thoughts running through his mind. Rapidly his thoughts are running through multiple ideas, but none of them have a solution to how to escape the death the creatures will soon deliver. Then again with the infection rates as high as ninety eight percent, no one has been able to figure a way around these attacks. The horrible situation for Bishop, which grows worse by the second.

As, he turns to his right to see the latest swarm attack, he sees Jones begin to wake up.

"Jones!"

Is all he can get out before he looks deeper into his face. He sees the same blank stare and unnatural bluish gray appearance. Jones groans for him in a deep growling voice.

"No fucking way! No!"

Ethan Bishop can't believe how far events spiraled out of control in just one day.

A creature bursts through the rear cargo window and is now inside the Suburban. Now, that the starving creatures actually, see a victim. Bishop is only feet away, the creature emits this strange tar colored ooze, which slobbers from it's mouth. Bishop gives a last look over to his former friend, Jones. In that split second his former best friend lunges at him. He's hit in the face hard with Jones shoulder. Blood immediately begins to flow from Bishop's cut eyebrow and lip. Sensing that the blood is in the air and feeding time is at hand. Both the Jones creature as, well as the creature from the rear get renewed energy.

Bishop punches at Jones, but his fists have no effect at all on the newly risen creature. As, he rears back to try to hit Jones again in the face, the drooling creature clamps down on Bishop's forearm. Tearing out a chunk from his flesh. He screams in horrible pain which fills the cabin. Yet, no one is around to even attempt to help him.

Blood pours out of his wound. It quickly, coats the tan cloth seats with blood. Jones locks down on his former friend's neck with vigor the creature yanks and pulls as the horrified, Bishop tries to beat the creature off of him. But, the punches have no effect, as he is physically in no shape to fight the two off from him.

Even though it didn't rip the flesh completely, out of Bishop's neck. It doesn't mean the damage isn't done. The skin is left hanging like a mud flap flapping in the wind. He tries to scream, but is unable to do so. Jones wastes no time biting down again on the throat. The bite crunches the wind pipes, as Jones pulls away to swallow the piece of flesh. The gapping wound collapses with blood, quickly filling the space where air is supposed to be.

As, Bishop quickly fades from life. The free flow of creatures inside of the suv is constant like the flow of the Mississippi River. Down it's entire range, finally emptying into the Gulf of Mexico. Bishop is choking on his own blood. He has not been able to bring oxygen into his lungs for over two minutes, now. The images that he's seeing are hazy and incomplete. Nothing makes sense inside of his mind. The sounds are muffled and he doesn't hear the female creature behind his bucket seat lurking.

The creature pounces on the near dead Bishop. It jumps towards him with half of it's body over the seat, as it clumsily tries to snap at the defenseless body of Bishop. The female creature lunges forward falling against the steering wheel. As, quick as a spring the creature regains it's position. Turning around to bite down on the exposed gaping hole in his throat. As, quick as the female ghoul takes to strike at Bishop. Is how long, it takes for him to die out of this life. Soon, he will be reborn into a new life minutes from now.

Over Highway 40, as far as the human eye can see is an area of the city taken over by these destructive and conquering creatures. Nowhere in this eight square mile radius is there any activity by humans. There are no cars traveling to work or shopping. No buses transporting it's occupants to their destination. As, far as humans are concerned they are now a extinct species in this Mississippi River town. But, even with our total and complete destruction the wildlife, still exist without harm. Birds fly and chirp in flocks overhead. While squirrels have free run of the trees as, well as the ground below. Yet, there are still pockets of humans hiding and existing in areas scattered throughout the city for now atleast.

23

1:54 P.M. OCTOBER 28, 2006

In the Benton Park section of South City. Joan Bennett wait's patiently sitting in her lounge chair. Constance, her granddaughter is the complete opposite of her grandmother. Pacing the hallway, looking outside the curtains. Then stomping her foot in frustration.

"Where could he be? There's got to be something wrong!" She says in a quick hurried fashion.

"Enough of that!"

Joan snaps, tired of her continual over blowing of each and every situation. But, also her nerves are frayed as well from this situation which is happening to her. Seconds after yelling at her granddaughter, Joan feels badly for it her. After all, she's really just worried about her brother.

"He'll be her shortly, you know it's a long walk from all the way down on Grand and Magnolia."

She says to reassure her scared and worried granddaughter.

Unexpectedly, Constance jumps up.

"That's it, I'm going to look for him!"

With that, she runs out of the front door. Exits the pathway that leads from Joan's front lawn. Towards the gates that split her neighborhood from the city. Then on Grand Boulevard.

Though Grand is a scene of total and complete chaos and destruction. Constance is forced to try and brave these challenging conditions. She desperately needs to find her brother, who she hasn't heard from now in over thirty minutes.

Nick sees an image he knows has to be his sister. He is still, well over a quarter mile away and without hesitation. He yells out to her from across Grand. He is standing outside the Lucky Girl nail salon on the sidewalk. She looks around to find the the familiar voice, but before she can locate him, she sees several groups of creatures. They are wandering around the Anheuser-Busch Eye Clinic, which is a half mile away. Cars, trucks, and buses are smashed and smoldering all over on Grand Boulevard. As, well as just about everywhere else the eye can see.

Constance can't believe the sights before her now. Seeing these horrible events separated by the TV is one thing. Yet, when actually forced to view such unpleasant sights most people spend a considerable amount of time in a state of shock. The same holds true for Constance, too. The group of creatures, which up to that point were patrolling the parking lot for victims. Quickly, they spot her and Nick, who was easily spotted by the creatures when, he yelled to his frightened sister.

For this is the first time that she has come face to face with the creatures. Quickly, noticing a man who was once like you or me. The creature is no human now which is why, it wonders away from the pack of creatures searching the parking lot. Towards it's next intended victim. The creature stalking towards Constance, was in it's human life, a forty-five year old school teacher at the high school. Which is not more than two miles from this location.

As, her eyes focus deeper on the creature, she notices why the man is no longer a school teacher. And is now one of the soon to be millions of walking dead. The creature's throat has been thoroughly ripped out. It stumbles in a herky jerky movement towards Constance, 'till the remainder of the creatures spot her, as well. Then with the knowledge that a feeding opportunity is just feet from them, the ghoul's leap into action. They all howl for Constance's flesh.

"AWAHHH!!!!!!"

Is the piercing sound the group makes, as the seven creatures hurry towards the guarded teen.

The school teacher ghoul screams as fourteen more creatures make a beeline towards Constance. The creatures are now sure and swift, as they chase in deadly pursuit of her.

Finally, Nick's voice gets over the chorus of screams and howls of the creatures to his sister.

"Get inside the gates!!!"

In, his statement to his terrified sister. Their Compton Heights neighborhood is surround by a seven foot wrought iron fence around the entire neighborhood. There are gates at all the entrances, so she enters. But, before she can safely pass through the gates and close them behind her. Five creatures quickly hurry towards her. He yells to his sister once again.

"Get back to the house!"

In helping to get the creatures away from her, it brings the heat to him. Nick yells and waves to attract the creatures. During this Constance runs from the gates, over to the first house on the left. There she crunches down and hides.

The bad news for Nick is that his diversion plan worked to well and now the creatures march with the sole intention of ripping him apart. Being no dummy on how to deal with the creatures. He wastes no time getting away from the open sidewalk. Nick runs onto Grand Boulevard dodging in between the wrecked and abandoned vehicles. The creatures are not quick on their feet at all.

With Nick using his brains and quickness, he is able to avoid the small band of creatures rather easily. He looks behind to see where the attacking creatures are. He's safe, as they're now behind him more than, twenty five feet. Coming around a wreck Bi-State bus, a ghoul pursuing Nick. Slips and smashes it's nasty face on the asphalt. Nick makes it to the opposite side of Grand. He quickly, closes the gates to this posh neighborhood behind him.

Constance comes out of her hiding spot the moment she sees that the person is indeed Nick.

"Nick!"

Is all she is able to get out before grabbing her brother and hugging him as tightly, as she can. Nick stands there in a uncomfortable stance for a second before, he then breaks away in a slick, macho guy way.

"We need to get to the house now!" He tells his shell-shocked sister.

"OK, Nick as long you're all right." She says, as she looks her brother over from head to toe. She can't find anything that looks out of place on him.

"Yeah Connie, I'm cool but we need to get out of sight. The sight of us drives them nuts! So, come on!"

"OK."

Is Constance's reply, as they run down the empty oak tree lined streets of this beautiful area. Small groups of creatures, many number less that six begin to wander from every conceivable area. From neighborhood streets to across the fresh mowed grounds of the Compton Heights Water Tower Park, which runs along Grand Boulevard. The creatures have a slow but purposeful walk. They make their way through the shambles of South City St. Louis. Their destination, the flesh of the Bennett's!

Nick and Constance pound on the heavy oak door to be let inside by their grandmother, Joan. What seems like an eternity to them, she finally unlocks the door. Nick pushes it open and the wrestling force pushes Joan back. She is stopped by the coat rack and the wall. Joan begins to say something to Nick, but is interrupted by him.

"We need to quickly get the house sealed shut. It won't be long before they hit here. Especially, since they saw us run here."

He says, as she stands there dumb founded that somehow they could get to her and her family.

"How many are there, Nick?"

Joan has no clue how bad things are out there and would have never thought what he's about to say is true.

"It's everyone, Grandma. No one is left!"

Joan and Constance want to say something but he said it all with that. Instead, he urges his sister to help him move the heavy 19th

Century cedar chest and slide it down the hardwood floors to block the front door from being burst open with ease. With Nick pushing for all he's worth as well as Constance, who is trying her best, but she just doesn't have the sheer grunt required to move such a bulky and heavy object. The cedar chest finally begins to slide and with momentum on their side, is pushed all the way down the hallway. Until the area rug gets bunched up underneath the little legs of the chest. Then with one final push, the chest is smacked tightly against the wall. As, quick as a jaguar, he hops halfway down the chest and with his hip, he pushes the chest firmly against the door.

Joan stands behind the action and doesn't seem to grasp what's going on. She's standing just a foot away but she seems to be a million miles away.

"Grandma! Are there any nails around here?"

His question goes unanswered and he asks again but in a much sterner way.

"Grandma, where are the nails!"

She seems really disoriented but manages to tell him where he might find the nails.

"They're out in the garage over by the work bench in those jars your grandfather used to store all the nails and screws in."

Joan's face shows the signs of sadness and loneliness that comes with the loss of someone, you have loved for so many years. Then suddenly they're taken one day from you, forever. Nick sees the sadness on his grandmother's face but, not knowing what to say and most importantly how to say, what he needs to. Instead, he turns around and walks out the back door towards the detached garage in the backyard, which has access to an alleyway.

While walking down the stone path to the garage, he hears the snap of a fallen tree branch. His neck jerks quickly to the left then back to the right. But, he sees that nothing is there. Even then he isn't ready to take any chances. Standing as firm as a statue, observing all the details which exist around him. Nothing though is moving except for a cool breeze which blows across the south against his face. Which brings a tear to his eye. What to do next? Is the message which runs up and down Nick's spinal cord between his eyes and his mind.

Now, after waiting thirty seconds and seeing nothing, Nick goes ahead. He begins to walk towards the garage. Inside of the garage are nails and supplies, he will need in order to seal up the entry points which cannot be secured with heavy objects. From the neighbors backyard comes the sound of rustling leaves and branches crackling, quickly sensing something. Nick is in shock and dismay as three creatures come staggering out from behind the shed next door. The soggy leaves under the creatures feet make a slushing sound, as they're dragged along the ground.

They continue to move towards him and the house. He is forced to abandon his quest for the nails and instead has to retreat back to the safety of the house. With long graceful strides, he is back at the steps leading into Joan's kitchen in less than five seconds. He flings the screen door, then the solid wooden door open. Then slamming the wooden door and locking it quickly. Even the chain is latched for more piece of mind.

Constance comes running in haste away from her grandma in the foyer towards the kitchen and her brother in the rear.

"Why, the hell did you just slam the door?"

As she steps in the kitchen, she sees her brother with the curtains pulled to the side in his right hand. She knows right away why, he slammed the door. It's an easy one to figure out. Paying no attention at all to the question coming from his sister.

His eyes instead only focus on the events which are happening just outside of the thin plane of window glass. His eyes and soon those of his sister, Constance fill with the horror of the disfigured walking dead. Making their way off of the main roads and through the alleyway. Finally, to the rear of their house. She hurries besides Nick to look out the window along side him. He doesn't even notice his sister next to him. As, soon as she sees what's out there, she too develops tunnel vision.

From the initial three creatures which startled Nick, there are now twelve as they clumsily stumble towards Joan's backyard. The group of creatures look confused and puzzled at how to overcome her five foot tall chain link fence. A male creature in it's early twenties tries with no success at all to jump on the fence and climb up it. Failing to scale the fence, the creature falls down hard onto the brick alley directly on it's hip. The creature staggers for a second before getting back up. Pounding on the chain links with it's fist in anger. The other creatures see that the ghoul failed and they look on at the fence tilting their lifeless heads trying to figure a way over. Inside, during this lull in action Nick pulls his sister away from the window.

"We need to seal this up windows and block that door!"

Nick says while he begins looking here and there for things, anything which could be used to block up the windows and doors. Keeping the creature back when they attack, Nick knows they will very soon.

"How, Nick? All the tools are out in the garage!"

"You think I don't know that Constance!"

He snaps at his sister in frustration and anger at being blocked off from the garage by the approaching creatures. But, soon he realizes her only concern is about him and his safety.

"I have to go out to the garage and get the hammer and nails!"

Constance is still stunned by his outburst at her.

"You can't do that!"

She snaps back at him. He ignores her stating.

"Just lock that door as soon as I am out."

Without further warning he runs out the door and she slams the door behind him. The lead glass shakes inside of the loose window frame. Quickly, she bolts the dead bolt. Looking out towards the garage where, he is struggling to open the padlock, which is preventing the two swinging doors from opening up for him. The first key on the ring doesn't unlock the doors for him.

On the opposite side of the fence, the creatures are getting worked up into a frenzy. The creatures pound and beat on the chain link fence, but so far, the fence is holding strong. A second and third key from the ring doesn't work either. Nick's starting to panic and rushing things too much. He drops the key ring on the ground, showing his impatience and anger, he slams his fist down against the concrete ground where the key's landed.

After hitting the concrete slab one good time the punch took the entire sting out of Nick's anger. He quickly gets himself under control and grabs the key ring from the ground. He tries again to unlock the doors. Unlike previous times, he succeeds this time. The padlock falls to the ground and he bolts inside the double doors. With no hesitation, he grabs a bag in which to store all the nails, hammer and supplies. By the handfuls, he loads the Eastman backpack with half inch, one inch, and two inch nails, are thrown into the pack. Along with a hand saw to cut anything that might need cutting inside. He was thorough but less than ninety seconds later, he exit's the garage. Looking over his shoulder and with the creatures only six feet away, it's then that he sees them begin to overload the fence.

The hollow aluminum tubes supporting the chain link mesh begin to bend. As, more and more creatures force their way on the bent fence. It arches farther and farther down towards the ground. Constance bangs on the lead glass window, trying her best to warn him of the approaching creatures. Yet, with all the noise that the creatures emit, and with panic running throughout his body. The sounds by her are the few that he doesn't hear. The realization that the creatures are not restricted, the odds of him getting back to the house alive and remaining human could be rough.

The creatures waste no time in going after him. The taste of his flesh to the creatures is an orgasmic feeling which they never want to end. Nick does not want to feel their effects, reacting he turns around and runs flat out back to the house. Inside the back porch Constance already has unlocked the dead bolt in anticipation of his return. Now that four creatures have penetrated the fence, Joan's backyard has a steady flow of creatures creeping from the alleyway, towards them. In a flash, he is close to the porch leading him to safety. Swiftly, he leaps the three steps, Constance swings the door open for him. He leaps in the the door, landing on his back. Instantly, he winces from landing hard with the backpack still on.

He rolls over one and half times. She slams the rear door shut and locks it without delay.

Nick is back up quickly yet is favoring his lower back. Limping over to the door just to make sure that she really locked it. He reaches down and grabs the backpack from the floor. Nick slings the navy blue pack on the bench. The pack knocks over a vase of flowers which Joan set up as a display for the back porch area. The mixture of water and bleach runs across the wood top then spills over the sides of the bench. Finally, falling on the linoleum floor. He does not pay a single second on the broken vase or the water which has fallen on the floor just feet away. He is busy opening up the pack and grabbing a handful of nails. He sets them on the cleared area of the table. He, then pulls out the hammer as well.

"Grab that board and hand it to me!" Nick barks at his sister.

Constance hurries over to the corner of the porch and grabs two planks that are being stored for the new floors, which were supposed to go down Thursday. He grabs the boards the second the creatures hit the door.

BOOM!

The sound of the impact makes Nick jump back and land on his already injured back again.

The attacking creatures more than startle Constance, who was carrying three more planks over to Nick. She never believed that once inside her house and out of the wide open and dangerous outside world, anything bad could happen to her. Crime victims rarely do think it could ever happen to them. But, bad, very bad things are happening to people who are good, bad and somewhere in between.

What is happening is no Biblical prophecy. No, the creatures are not seeking out the wicked. They are not judging the damned to be put to death. No, this is a man-made disaster. It was brought by man's own hand. His own greed for profit's from the next wonder drug. Combine all this with his lust for that one miracle drug which might not cure cancer or AIDS. But, your toe nails won't be yellow anymore or the one that will allow men to be able to achieve erections all the way into their nineties. No, it is man's fault and the residents of St. Louis are paying a very high price for that greed.

Nick, Constance and Joan are paying the ultimate price as well.

"Help me now!"

Nick yells to his sister who ran behind him towards doorway. In the space between the back porch and the kitchen.

Reluctantly his sister comes back over to assist her brother, as he frantically tries to hammer the boards. He is doing so, at the top corners of the door at a slant, where he can nail directly into the door frame. As, well as in the door itself to strengthen it as much as possible.

"You gotta hold the board still, I can't hold it and hammer it at the same time."

"All right, Nick, I will!"

She yells to him yet, grabs the board from him anyway. The back porch has four huge bay windows. Nick is hammering the boards over the last of the corners.

Then the worst sound imaginable to them happens. The sound of broken glass. A brick is thrown from the flower box. The brick flies through the window smashing into the plaster wall facing the kitchen. After making the indentation, it falls along with the broken bits of plaster fall, which heavily to the ground. Constance screams and Joan comes running from the living room. Then into the kitchen to see what exactly is going on. Her eyes immediately go to the gaping hole in her back window. Joan isn't at all aware of the creatures who are just mere feet from killing not only her but also her grandchildren, as well.

"What happened to my door?"

Joan demands to know. She doesn't even seem to notice that Constance and Nick are quickly working trying to keep the creatures from breaking down the door. Which the creatures will do in a manner of moments, if it's not secured properly.

Nick looks back at yells at his grandmother.

"Get out of here! Those damn things are beating the door down!"

She looks surprised, as if your telling a child there's no presents for Christmas this year.

Joan stands there, talking to herself. She's confused, not sure what she should be doing. Nick starts to yell at her again but Constance jumps in before he can get out anymore other than.

"Grandma…"

"Get in the living room if you can't get your mind clear and actually help us!"

Joan hears the message from her granddaughter and scrambles back through the kitchen and away from her grandchildren. It's that split second distraction which allows the horde of creatures to gain the upper hand. With a thud, the back door cracks around it's brass hinges. The door splinters and sends a large six-inch sliver of wood to protrude out towards them both. The door is broken off it's hinges and is floating in limbo because it is still nailed to the door frame. Nick tries to hammer up a long board across the middle section of the door. He's hoping that this board can some how keep the twenty creatures out, who hungrily pound on the broken door.

The moans and groans, as the creatures continue their march through the back door are enough to frighten anyone with a pulse. It makes you want to flee from this situation, as quick as possible. The creatures smack and beat on the brick walls outside. Sounds of boom and clang resonate inside of the porch. Nick manages to get two nails in the right and left sides of the three feet long board. It's a good brace, as they face a fierce onslaught from the creatures. These creatures are definitely not unintelligent, as they can make decisions based on what they witness in their environment.

The creatures witnessed how effective that the brick through the window actually was. A white ghoul in it's early forties with it's eye socket completely void of an eye. Also, exposed from the wound is bits of stringy deep red muscle tissue that was forcibly ripped out by another of those deadly creatures. The ghoul misses grabbing the brick at first, due to it's lack of depth perception. It's hand moves clumsily around the flower box 'till it finally grabs what it wants.

Standing up and with some aiming, the brick goes flying towards the besieged house. The glass from the window explodes. A second brick crashes through and breaks a lamp that was being stored on the back porch. The scene on the porch is no longer a serene place to relax during a beautiful fall afternoon. It is more like what the residents of Berlin must have felt when the Allies bombarded the German city during World War Two.

With two big holes in the windows, there is now a major opening which in time the creatures will figure out. These openings are a perfect way to get inside and obtain their prey. But, right now, the creatures are concentrating on the door with all their energy. They know now, that right behind the door are their prey: Nick and Constance. They want their flesh! With the creatures piled up four deep on the porch steps, the creatures pound on the door. With each blow, Nick's center brace shakes and loosens-up that much more.

"What now, Nick?"

Constance shouts out while he continues to nail another 2x4 to cross the first board and make an X-type pattern.

"Hold this. We need this second board up there."

Constance listens and holds the board. But, the creatures are still pushing on the door. Even with the cross board, the door is leaning in towards them.

The brother and sister team look at each other, it's written on their faces, they both know something terrible is about to happen.

"We gotta get in the main house. They'll break this door down anytime now!" Nick blasts over the hectic noise of the creatures.

"They'll get us there too, Nick!" She says as her mind sinks deeper into despair.

"We gotta try, we just can't stay here and let those damn things get us, now can we? Let's go!"

And with that, he grabs a hold of his sister's hand with his and they both hurry through the kitchen and into the living room where Joan is standing. She is looking out her front window. She's witnessing an entirely new Compton Heights than she's ever seen before in her eighty four years.

The creatures in the rear have attracted some fellow competitors. There are now sixty more creatures marching over the lawns. Through the streets and towards the Bennett house at 3665 Victoria Street.

"Are there any of those things out there, Grandma?"

Constance asks Joan, but she does not even turn around to acknowledge her granddaughter, she just answers her in a quite monotone voice.

"Yes, dear they are everywhere."

Nick jumps in and asks her exactly how many of them are outside. At first she doesn't respond to him.

"Grandma!" He shouts.

She snaps out of it and responds

"A hundred or so give or take." Joan says to her grandson.

"Fuck!"

Is the only expression, he can utter. He knows what that news means. The odds are against them and it doesn't look good at all.

"What now, Nick"

Constance asks, as a she sits down cross legged on the hardwood floor next to him. He is somber and introspective as, he stands up pulling away as his sister desperately tries to hold on to his arm.

"Nothing!"

The answer to her question is not and was not what she was expecting to hear from her brother.

"What?!"

She says so shocked and sad at the same time. Inside she is furious with him. Even if this attack by the creatures is the end, how could he just give up like this? How could someone that, I admire and love, so much not want to fight not only for himself but also for Grandma and me. This is her reaction to her brother's statement.

"There's really just no way, Constance, they're everywhere." He sees the utter disappointment in her sunken body language.

"Look, if you have a plan tell me now cause, I don't see anyway out of here."

"So, what are we just waiting here to die?"

Nick doesn't answer Constance and instead walks over to his grandmother. Putting his arm around her. He walks his her out of the living room and up the second floor stairs to get her away from the first wave of attack at least.

She says aloud in a hazy state of confusion.

"It'll all work out for the best, you'll see."

That was the last sentence which Joan Bennett ever spoke to anyone for the short time remaining of what was her very long life. Joan walks the rest of the way up the staircase by herself. Nick comes back down the stairs. His sister is standing at the window looking at the forthcoming horde. The group outside have steadily increased their numbers over the last five minutes from ten to the better part of on hundred!

Their collective hum is overwhelming. Like a plague of attacking locusts. They hunger for the flesh of the living they know are inside of the house. For those inside they know there's no escape from the dead which seek them. The creatures will not stop until they are completely destroyed.

"Why did you put her up there?" She quips at him.

"You know why."

Nick's somber reply to his sister. The hum of the creatures has became a roar. Nick and Constance brace for the initial impact of the attack. The creatures beat and claw at the door and windows which flank either side of the metal door. Fist after thunderous fist is launched with ferociousness by an attacker that has no intention of just scaring you. No, they seek total and complete destruction of you and everything in this society. The high intensity glass is taking tremendous loads of force. They are both helpless to escape now.

BAMM!

Quickly, a crowd of ten creatures pierce the door. Flooding inside the house, so tightly at first that the clog doesn't move at all. Then the instant the creatures have some space between themselves. They're off and instantly the disgusting creatures occupy the entire first floor of the house.

Constance and Nick are split apart for the first time since the creature attack began. She flees to the left of the staircase while he opts to go through the kitchen, escaping to the back porch. Nick observes the failure of his plan the instant he turns the corner from the kitchen into the porch's door frame. The creatures have overpowered the back door and have trickled into the now empty room. Also there are, the throngs of creatures which still occupy the back yard. Thus cut off any escape in that direction that he might have hoped for. He's trapped and there's no way out. He desperately flings himself into the creatures, which are taken by surprise at seeing an actual living human.

Nick elbows a tall and stringy ghoul in the stomach knocking the creature completely off balance. The clumsy creature falls through the half broken window landing right on it's back. Instantly, the ghoul stops moving. Nick gets past that ghoul but two others close in quickly on him. He tries to retreat back into the interior of the house, yet the creatures pursuing continue to stalk him with vigor.

Then as he enters back through the doorway and in the kitchen, his eyes for an instant fill with the chaos and destruction to this once peaceful and beautiful home. The attacking creatures have sacked the home. Nick goes further inside attempting to get away from the creatures that are coming after him from the rear. He looks over to the left side of the house to Constance's bedroom.

To the right beside the downstairs bathroom, he sees his sister. Lying motionless with vicious chunks of flesh ripped completely from her body. On the floor, blood has drained from her wounds. Soaking her clothes that weren't already destroyed. She lost so much blood that is, now starting to soak into the grain of the wood flooring.

Nick's mind sinks deep into sadness but that sensation doesn't last long. A female ghoul lunges for him snapping deep in his bicep. He is thrown in intense pain, as he tries to shake the creature off from his arm. But, these creatures are like pit bulls. They won't let go, as long as their teeth are sunk into flesh. As, he turns to swing the ghoul off, three additional creatures immediately swarm him knocking him down to the hardwood floor. The sting of his head smacking the wood flooring is nothing compared to the throbbing pain in his arm. On the ground the creatures make up for their lack of coordination pouncing on the stunned and injured Nick. He tries his best to fight them off but the creatures are just too numerous and rabid for him.

In, fact there was no way, he never stood a chance against the onslaught from the creatures bites. Their hungry mouths penetrate through the left side of his neck while simultaneously, his ear is bitten hold of. As, the creature jerks away from him, the flesh tears down the side of his neck like taffy. Nick screams and shakes in terror and agony. But, his shrills are mute and quiet compared to what a person without a ripped out throat could do. Even with the fatal bite delivered, the creatures don't relent. A pancake size piece of his right neck is yanked out, a gush of blood comes bubbling to the surface of his body. His eyes close for the final time. His mind releases the thoughts feelings, dreams, fears and pain that once occupied the mind of this person named Nicholas Bennett.

24

2:06 P.M. OCTOBER 28, 2006

With their squad car failing on them rapidly and Kingshighway becoming more impassable the farther they venture north. Inside the car Darryl asks his partner.

"What's our game plan?" Barton looks in the side mirror to the scene behind them

"We had one back there?!" He asks his best friend and partner, quizzically.

"No, but I thought you might have hatched one by now!"

Darryl jokes back, the two men seem to have accepted this shitty situation. Then made peace with their fate.

"We mine as well abandon this ship, right"

Darryl asks knowing they'll have to anyway cause the squad car is all used up.

"Hell, let's dump this piece of shit then."

With that statement they disembark on Kingshighway before the Viaduct begins. It spans over the railroad tracks and industrial park below. Before the two leave their squad car behind for good, they clean out the items that they'll need. The pump action shot gun, the remaining ammo that's left. Most telling of their situation is they take their handcuffs and radio equipment off. They know they're not making any more arrests. Or, calling for backup to come and take the suspects away. They are on their own. No one is coming to help.

St. Louis is now in many ways like an old west town. Fitting for a town which bridged the gap from the east to the west, during America's expansion west. The town that facilitated this now resembles a wide open and lawless frontier town. Not a once vibrant metropolis. The noise of the creatures has dropped. Nothing is moving anywhere within sight right now. The creatures, the two left to the south are not making their presence felt.

Darryl and Barton desperately hope to God they don't find their way back to them. Then with the thought of more of the creatures ahead of them causes Darryl's to tingle with millions of goose bumps forming across his arms. He has been on the force twelve years. Has been shot at five times. During these twelve years, he has seen numerous fellow officers killed during the line of duty. Never once during any of these incidents did he ever questions his loyalty to the force. During the last encounter, he had these thoughts run through his head.

"If I get a clear path, I am getting out of here, I am taking it! Screw, Barton if he isn't here when I am ready to go then that's his problem, not mine." Is what Darryl was thinking back there.

It's funny how in an extremely stressful situation, people morph and change into someone, they themselves would not recognize in a normal setting.

Inside he fells like shit for thinking about leaving his partner behind to be literally eaten alive by those God Damn things. His emotions now overwhelm him, he shouts out loud.

"Fuck them!"

With that he kicks the road hard with his steel toe boot. Barton notices this rare outburst of emotions from his partner. He knows something really wrong is bothering him. Because usually, Darryl is always calm, cool and collected.

"What's wrong with you?"

He asks in a joking manner but Darryl's mood has changed drastically from a minute ago when they were laughing about leaving the squad car behind.

"Nothing, everything, what does it matter?"

"What's up with you all the sudden?"

Darryl goes to walk away from him with out answering. Barton grabs him, spinning Darryl back around towards himself. Face to face, he asks again what's bothering him. This time only in a much harsher tone.

"Don't grab me, like that again!"

He lets him go, as he doesn't want to fight with him, he just wants to know what's getting his best friend.

"Lets just get going, all right?!"

"Fine by me."

Underneath his breath Barton quips.

"Asshole!"

"I think it'll be best avoid Kingshighway for now on, as well as any of the bigger roads. What do you think about taking the railroad tracks out of here? It's' got to be a hell of a lot better out in the county."

Darryl asks trying to change the mood between him and Barton. But, he doesn't make any reply to his partner. Instead, he starts walking underneath the Viaduct to get to the railroad tracks which lay underneath Kingshighway Boulevard.

Darryl follows a step or two behind him, knowing when it's best to give way. Letting his partner have time enough to cool down. He knows for a fact that the incident is entirely his fault, but he just could not admit to Barton why he was so upset. Barton decides that heading west on the tracks will be the safest way to get out this explosive situation. That's an easy call to make as going east would bring you right through the heart of Downtown St. Louis. Before you cross the Martin Luther King Bridge finally entering Illinois. The crossing, brings you into a relatively rural environment with miles of entering Illinois.

To their west lies the populated suburban towns of Shrewsbury, Crestwood and Sunset Hills. Even though these towns don't pack the sheer numbers of the city of St. Louis, their populaces live in high-density urban areas. So, it's the best of a bad situation and they head west. Both know that not one part of this trip, will be easy. But, they really have much of a choice. Their only hope for escape is that for one reason or another, the creatures have moved away from the railroad tracks to somewhere, anywhere but here.

There's not much left underneath of the Viaduct on Kingshighway anymore. Most of the big manufacturing companies left years before. In there place went smaller companies, dealing in areas such as medical records keeping and other data processing tasks. Apparently, the building's are vacant of creatures, which is odd. Because the parking lot is filled with over thirty cars. It's obvious that at least thirty to fifty people were here at some point during this afternoon.

Barton and Darryl are aware at any instant an overwhelming number of creatures could break from any spot. Descending upon the lone police officers in a surprise attack. They proceed with extreme caution and vigilance as they maneuver down this potential hotbed of destruction. With each step they take, their boots disturb the rocks below that are laid over the railroad tracks to reduce the vibrations from the trains passing by. Right now both officers, simply wish that these damn things would just disappear.

Crunch and crackling is the sounds which pops from the sparkly rocks as they hit the railroad tracks and the huge, railroad ties that support the rails.

Clank!

It's the sound of a wooden object being knocked over. Did it happen by somebody or something? Or was it just the wind?

Darryl and Barton freeze as tightly as the metal rails below them. Both men wait in anticipation, yet nothing moves. Is it possible the wind simply blew the object over? Or, could one of those creatures be lurking out of sight, waiting for Barton and Darryl to stroll past then.

BAMM!

Attack and destroy them when the two men would be caught totally caught off guard. No, their guns are drawn and ready to fire at any creature which might pop out at them. They continue to stalk down the tracks to the west, not taking anything for granted. Slowly, and cautiously the two move toward the target that Barton heard moments ago. Barton quickly turns towards the BJC medical records division building. Since the initial noise nothing else has been heard. Going on through out Darryl's mind is.

"It's' gotta be just the wind."

"Nothing's here."

Daryl barks to his partner. Still they both proceed closer and closer towards the building. Both men's nerves are on edge, as they creep closer and closer. Still there's nothing to be seen. As, they both enter into the outer hallway which leads to the interior of the building. The wind blows a strong gust as the air is forced around the corridors of the building. When a person is pressed into a situation such as this, your mind begins playing tricks on you. A person can think that, they hear things creeping up behind them. But in reality nothing is really there. Barton's mind is playing these very same cruel jokes on him, right now.

"There's something behind us on the tracks."

Runs through his mind. Quickly, he turns around with his gun aimed right at the heart of whatever might be behind, him. But, he sees that nothing was ever behind him. Darryl who has continued to go deeper in the building, he reacts to his partner actions.

Never turning his back from the building, Darryl yells over to Barton.

"Nothing. I thought I heard something behind me, but it's nothing."

He turns back around covering the rear for his partner. Still, neither man spots anything. Now that they're inside of the records building up to this point, they have found nothing, so far. No bodies, or blood, not even signs of distress. The lack of evidence that something is inside has caused them both to relax a little. Both men hoister their 9 mm Smith and Wesson side arms. The lights that illuminate the building are turned off, it's extremely dark inside the offices and around the building. The only light comes from MagLite's which both men carry.

"What do you wanna do, Darryl?"

He asks not sure himself on what he wants to do with this strange situation.

"Let's see if there might be anything here we could use."
Gesturing his head in agreement.
"Yeah, I could use something to hold this damn shotgun."
Barton says to Darryl.
"What do you think this is, a K-Mart or something?"
Both men get a good quick laugh but are sure they do not get too loud.
"Well, let's get going then and get this done with!"
Darryl tells Barton, as he opens a office door leading to a room labeled 001A Records Division 1995-2000.

Inside the pitch-black room, you can make out the outlines of desks and computers along with cabinet after cabinet filled with patients medical history. Barton shines his flashlight into the dark empty room. A relief to him, nobody is in here. With that worry behind him, he enters the room. Darryl focuses his search for the light switch. Six feet down the wall on his right he, finds the control panel and turns on the lights. When the lights come on, is when they see on the floor below, the mutilated bodies of the workers. Along the walls are the bloody hand trails of the victims, as they staggered to their gruesome death.

Both men redraw their side arms, not wanting to take any chances in this scenario. But, these dead people are not moving. Both men continue to go deeper inside the office to make sure nothing is lurking in the rear.

Darryl takes the left while Barton swings right. The smell of the dead bodies has already begun to permeate the room.

As, Barton moves swiftly to the right, his eyes glance over to the dead bodies lying mangled on the floor. As, he looks away, he thinks to himself.

"Damn, I wish Darryl would have never turned the lights on. I can't stand looking at them. They're just torn to shreds. It looks like the floor of a slaughter house."

The sight and smell of death is starting to get to him.

"I don't see anything back here, it's clear!" Darryl yells out.

He's already finished and his partner knows, he will need to get his butt into gear and finish checking his area. Finally, he finishes checking his side.

"Yeah, this side is all clear, too."

Barton and Darryl come together to search for anything that they might find useful to take for their journey. Nothing is around except some blood soaked purses and those little shoulder messenger bags that have become popular in the last few years. There's nothing here worth sticking your hand in all that blood for, the two men agree.

"Let's get movin', huh?" Darryl asks.

"Yeah, I think it's best if we do!"

They exit the building hoping to never see a scene like that one again. Still the two of them have that gut feeling that something about this place just isn't right. Yet, neither of them really wants to learn the truth, which lurks hidden from their sight.

"What now, Darryl?"

His partner asks, as they survey the scene around the records building.

"Let's just get the hell out of here, we need to get out of the county before night falls."

He says to Barton, who is looking at him with a disbelieving look on his face.

"There is no way we're going to come close to getting even halfway out to the county by the time it gets dark!"

Barton, who is really starting to show signs of stress, says to him.

"Then let's get goin' now then!" Darryl quips back to him.

"Fine." He says in a sulking voice.

Towards the railroad tracks they begin walking at a slant. Back at the building, a faint sound emerges. Neither Darryl or Barton hears it. They continue to walk as, they reach the tracks. The sound grows progressively louder finally catching Darryl's ear. He jumps like a startled child, turning completely around to see where the noise is coming from. What, he and Barton see drills fear from they're heads; straight through to their toes.

The torn and mangled bodies from inside the room are now joined by four other creatures. They are not in the damaged state that the seven office workers are in. Their first thought is obvious.

RUN!

But, if they do the creatures will follow them. As, well their moans and screams will draw all the creatures from the entire southwestern edge of St. Louis City to be on alert.

They must stay and destroy or be destroyed by these creatures. Darryl has his 9 mm hand gun with two clips left. Twenty bullets the same goes for Barton. Along with his 12-gauge shotgun and fourteen cartridges. This group of creatures don't seem as coordinated, as the other creatures they've have encountered. As, with humans the level of coordination varies between individual to individual. It must come down to competence of the leadership and the ability to communicate amongst the members.

The creatures stagger towards Barton and Darryl. Both men have their guns aimed at the creatures waiting for the right second to fire and blow their grotesque head's apart like a cantaloupe. The seven creatures from the office continue clumsily toward the two officers. Their bodies are unsteady, as they walk over the railroad beams. The remaining four that initially joined with them have backed-off. They are now standing still and not advancing forward. Barton and Darryl are forty feet away from the seven, but their still too far to fire with accuracy they desire. The creatures pace quickens, as they hunger to experience their first taste of human flesh.

Now at twenty five feet, Darryl fires.

BAMM! BAMM! BAMM!

Three shots hit one creature, who's entire face was void of flesh exposing bone is hit. The bullets smack, rip and tear into the skull of the ghoul as, it falls to the ground. The remaining six creatures pay no attention and continue pursuing their goal. Still the four remain behind, yet to join the pursuit.

Barton fires, too.

BAMM! Shot one is off target, but manages to hit the staggering ghoul in the shoulder. With that wound, the ghoul losses a step. But, immediately regains it's pace and starts it's pursuit again.

BAMM! Shot two clips of the ghoul's head near it's ear.

"FUCK!"

BAMM! BAMM! Shots three and four hit the ghoul in the top of the skull. Sending huge sticky chunks of blood and skull flying high in the air. The creature falls hitting the ground with a thud. Again with, a fallen sidekick, it does not phase the other creatures. They continue marching, they just keep moving towards them both.

The creatures movements change. They're moving fast now like rats off a sinking ship. Their only ten feet away and both men are startled. The officers are forced to retreat several feet back attempting to gain a better position over the creatures.

Now, both men are off balance, as the five creatures advance. The second group of creatures advances aggressively towards the two officers. When they spot the second group of four coming towards them. They are once again forced to retreat even further west.

The second group played their hand perfectly, they sacrificed the expendable ones. Fooled Barton and Darryl into a false sense of security. They then pounced on their opportunity. Now, the two men are running for their lives. The creatures tricked them perfectly and with nowhere to retreat to, Barton and Darryl have little chance to escape.

The creatures never tire out. In many ways they are the perfect machine. They can think on their own, don't require programming codes or electricity like robots. It seems that somewhere in the evolution from human to creature. That somehow, their brains were deprogrammed of the part, that receives the messages from the body that says.

"Hey, my muscles are over extended and tired."

Yet, they do share one weakness of humans. The need for replenishing their hunger with food. That is exactly what Darryl and Barton are. Simply stated, there's nothing personal or vindictive about their actions just instinctive. But, I doubt Darryl or Barton view it in this context, as they struggle for their survival.

As, they come across the Viaduct, they see a shooting range housed inside a large prefab aluminum building. It's not a great refuge, but at least it will provide a chance for them to regroup. Then they can attempt to try another plan of attack against the creatures. Darryl and Barton both know they have to come up with a fail safe plan.

They were outsmarted once, that can't happen again. As, they reach the building, they duck behind the corner. They are now looking onto Manchester. Both men are exhausted, drenched in sweat, and winded. There's no time to worry about being out of breath. That will have to wait, the approaching creatures won't.

Attempting to inhale as much air as his lungs can, Darryl tries to explain his plan.

"How about this….? I stay at this end, you go to the far end and as they come around we can line those fuckers up!"

Barton nods his head in agreement.

"Sounds good enough. Let's do it!"

They face each other hitting their fists together knowing this may be the final time they do, so.

"Come on! Let's kick some zombie ass!!"

Darryl yells. Barton advances to his position. His eyes scan every inch to make sure that, he doesn't accidentally bump into a ghoul. The coast is clear, he slides feet first into the wet dirt scattered with patches of grass and weeds.

Darryl sticks his head out and gives him the thumbs-up. Then both men dart back to lie and wait for them to advance. Sitting with his gun in hand, Darryl thinks just how much he loves Sofia, his wife. How he desperately wants to see her once more but deep inside his heart, he knows he never will.

Barton on the other hand is thinking only of the revenge, he can take out on the creatures. It won't be long before, he can give them his all. The creatures approach quickly with the damaged one's still in front. The creatures which charged forward have backed off once again. They have flanked two each to the left and the right. Darryl and Barton have lost sight of those creatures.

The five creatures from the office advance strongly, as they yell out a war cry. The moans and cries alert both men to their position.

"They're a hundred feet away."

Yells Darryl. He can't tell if Barton heard him or not over the noises of the creatures.

They scurry towards Darryl first. He holds steady 'till the creatures get within range that his handgun will be effective. Seconds feel like hours, while he waits for the fight of his life. They come running as fast as their bodies will allow. They're not as fast as the four who have split up, but they're pretty quick.

They continue towards him and he knows, that this is it. There is no way out for either man. It's win or lose. The stakes are their lives.

Darryl is the first to fire.

BAMM! BAMM! He misses both of his shots. The creatures make hard targets as, they are running towards him.

Barton meanwhile hears the two shots and wonders how his partner is doing with the creatures. Barton shouts.

"Damn it! I need to be over there!"

But, for the plan to work, he needs to stay put, doing his part for the plan to have maximum impact.

BAMM! A third shot echoes loudly off the surrounding building. This one finds Darryl's desired target. At roughly forty feet away, a ghoul's head rips open from the bullet. It enters straight thru the skullcap and exit's, the rear of the skull. Brain matter spews out. The creature slumps down on the ground just a few feet from of the railroad tracks. Four shots so far with six left in the clip and only one clip left. Every shot left is critical. Darryl does not have a single bullet to waste. The pressure is on and he feels every bit of it.

BAMM! BAMM! Two more are out of the chamber, hitting a white female ghoul. One in the shoulder and the other thru the neck. There's a gapping hole in it's neck. But, still the creature continues forward with the injury. The only sign anything is wrong, is the drawing noise through the ravaged hole in it's throat.

"Fuck!"

Darryl yells out in frustration at using so many bullets and killing just one creature, so far.

"Wait 'till they get closer then shoot, got it?!"

He says this to himself. He stands up and braces himself against the aluminum building for some additional support and waits. The two creatures that went to the right along Manchester are now waiting hungrily for their opportunity to feed upon Barton and Darryl. It looks good for them, they're in position to strike out at both men. Neither of the humans have a clue, as to what awaits them.

Hiding across the road in a factory which produces metal castings. The creature's can see Darryl beginning to be over loaded with the four ghoul's that are left. The creatures now are only twenty feet away. Darryl fires one, two, and three rounds, emptying the clip, Barton hears it too.

The creatures begin to advance even quicker now. Darryl pops his last clip in and fires.

WHAM!

Seven feet from him the bullet splatters the forehead of a black female ghoul the instant before tearing him apart. Caught by the creatures, the final three creatures grab him and tosses him to the dirt. Quickly, he escapes their grip while attempting to get back to his feet. They vigorously paw and grab a hold of him. He tries his best to fight them off, but feels like he is in quick sand. Desperate to get loose, he rears back and kicks a female ghoul square in the chest, sending it backwards. Darryl jumps to his feet, and grabs his gun. As, he struggles with a second creature. He fires off a shot causing the ghoul's head to explode like an egg that has just been hit with a hammer. Darryl has two more to deal with. Thinking that all the creatures have been dealt with he yells for Barton.

"Barton get this damn thing off me!"

Barton flies around the corner. Meanwhile, behind a group of parked semitrailers in the gravel parking lot, there are two fresh creatures. Barton's eyes fill with horror and disbelief.

"Not more!"

Caught of guard, he is knocked hard against the shooting range's wall. A creature on his right side chomps down on his flaying forearm.

"Awah!"

He screams in pain. Blood gushes the inside of the creature mouth and begins to spill from it's lips. The creature's grip is unbreakable for Barton, he can't force it to let go. During the tussle, the creature's force him to the ground. He's on his back, completely exposed to the punishment, the creatures can dish out. Darryl, hears his partner and best friend. Grabs his attacker by it's shoulders and manages to throw the ghoul off him. It hits hard against the wall. He doesn't wait around to deal with the ghoul. Instead, he quickly runs to help Barton.

When he gets to his partner, his eye's fill with horror, as Barton is up against the wall at an angle which exposes his entire side. Darryl notices bright red blood running down his arm, and down the metal wall behind him. The creatures ravaged mouth is dripping with his blood, too.

"Barton!"

Is all Darryl can get out as, he joins the struggle to free him from the creature's deadly embrace. The creatures are formidable opponents and both men are experiencing first hand. They are in fact not as strong as a typical 5'8", one hundred and fifty pound red blooded American male but they move like boiled spaghetti noodles. The creatures just twist and bend with you as you struggle against them.

Darryl hits the creature that is tearing into Barton's arm over the back of it's skull with the butt of his 9 mm Smith & Wesson. The creature's head split's open and it breaks it's grip long enough for Barton to free himself.

The wound is bad, but not yet bad enough to be life threatening. Barton kicks at the creature managing to knock it off it's feet. Darryl aims and fires from near point blank range. The creature's skull implodes from the bullet and with it, a trail of brain matter oozes out, as the ghoul slumps down to the ground. Seeing their opportunity to feed upon humans slipping away, the final two creatures from across the north side of Manchester move into action. They come running, as fast as any human at full speed. Darryl sees them coming but can't react since his hands are full fighting with the creature.

Barton is in even worse shape, he is growing weaker from not only the loss of blood. But, inside his blood stream is pumping the virus which has caused this outbreak to move so swiftly through his veins, taking effect. The remaining creature from the office comes into the fray as well. The more advanced creature's focus their attack on the weaker of the two men, Barton. The quickness and precision which the creatures strike on him is amazing. His mind is lost in a fever of confusion, he is unaware of the attack until he is knocked head first onto the ground.

Darryl can't help his troubled friend as, the ghoul from the office struggles to force his gun from him. The second ghoul recovers from being kicked to the ground. Now storming towards Darryl. The aggressive ghoul focuses in on his waving arm and bites it!. The bite crunches through the flesh. Blood begins to bubble up to the surface. Striking at the ghoul, he hits it in the face. The impact is substantial but the ghoul comes right back. Their efforts are overwhelming and the creatures begin to devastate with deadly force.

Barton lies on the ground, much of him is already a creature and what is human can not comprehend what is happening to his body. The haze, he is experiencing is thick, his mind does not respond to the trauma placed on his body by the creatures. The only feeling, he has left is being incredibly hot. The fever inside is forcing his body to sweat profusely. The creatures continue to feed upon him even though he is *'one of them.'* This is a good chance for them to replenish their need. It's an easy feeding opportunity. Something no successful predator would pass.

The creatures take turns biting down on his neck, filling their mouths with Barton's dying flesh. Darryl looks at his friend one final time. He passes from the living to be reborn a creature of the dead.

Darryl has his own problems to deal with. He can't shake the creature from the office off of him. The furious creature continues to shred his left arm. He's desperately trying to kick it off but instead, he's knocked down to the ground. The ravenous creature jumps on top of him. With vicious tearing bites, the creature has him barely hanging to life. The lower ranking creature tries to come and share in the bounty. The more advanced creature jumps up from Darryl snapping at the intruder. Obviously, it, is not willing to share it's meal.

25

3:09 P.M. OCTOBER 28, 2006

The creatures numbers are continuing to add up outside the besieged supermarket. Thankfully for the people inside, none have tried to gain access. For the inhabitants inside, it's been quiet outside the store for the last thirty minutes. In this time, everyone has relaxed as much as possible. This loll in action has given everyone a pause to think about something other than the invasion. Some people have had a quick bite to eat while others continue to peak out the windows curious to see what is happening outside. While others still try to use the now defunct telephone network. Their attempts to reach family and friends via their mobile phones have failed, as well. Communication networks are apparently down or over loaded. For now nothing is works anywhere within the city. Whatever the case may be, the fact remains nothing is working.

"Is anyone getting any kind of news at all?"

Asks a white woman who is eating some Ritz crackers and downing a 20 ounce bottle of Pepsi.

"No, you know that! You might wanna try and save some of that junk food for later. We don't know how long we all might be stuck here."

The Bosnian store manager says. The woman gives him a dirty look and goes back to her twelve year-old overweight son, who is also eating junk food.

This prompts the manager to speak to the group.

"Look everyone, we just can't sit around and eat. We need to conserve what we have. So, lets take it easy."

Just as he finishes, Janis the heavy set black woman backs up the manager for the first time.

"Ya'll need to take it easy. We might be in here for a long damn time. Cause, I don't see those damn things goin' away anytime soon."

A collective. "Yeah, that's a good idea." Goes up from the group. Everyone knows that this situation might last a long time.

"Well, does anyone have a plan? I haven't heard anything about what we should be doing."

Asks a mid thirties black man.

The businessman attempts to turn the group from uncertain panic to being a group that bonds together feeling confident and strong.

"It looks like were on our own. Whatever we do, we need to figure it out soon before the situation dictates it to us. The power is continuing to cut in and out. We still don't know how much time, we have left."

During, the past thirty minutes electricity across the city has began to faultier. The power grid in the city is very reliable, but it seems at the central switching facility, that the lack of technicians tending to the situation has placed great strain on the all ready taxed grid. Some parts of the city have already gone dark and no longer are receiving any electricity. Slowly each area of the town is being shut down and at this time it is, not clear if, the electricity will ever return.

It seems as though the group wants to be unified. It doesn't appear that there is a designated leader. This could be a good thing since no one is asserting dominance over the other members.

"What we need to do is organize the food into two groups. Perishable and nonperishable. The power could go in time, so we need to use the meats, fresh vegetables and bread before it goes to waste. Also, we need to stock up on the water, it could go off at any time."

The businessman says.

"Then lets do it!" States Janis.

"Ok, two groups. First one for the meat, go and remove it then put it in the freezers. We need that food to last. Second, get the vegetables and fruit's. Those need to be eaten within the next couple of days."

The store manager says and with that everyone breaks into two's. With their hands and arms overloaded with packs of meat the Victor and the businessmen enter aisle seven were the frozen foods are located.

"What do you think is happening out there?"

Victor asks, as he tries to seek some answers to all the chaos swirling around him.

"I am not sure, I doubt anyone knows for certain."

He says trying to portray a sense of calmness to the young man, who he still has yet to tell his name, too.

"By the way, I am Ted."

Victor is taken back, as everyone here is guarded. Not sharing any personal information, including their names.

"Oh, I am Victor, as you can see, I work here."

He tells Ted in a slightly embarrassed tone realizing his name tag, on his uniform clearly identifies him, as an employee of Food World.

"Yeah, thought your name sounded familiar."

Both smile, as they continue to carry meat toward the frozen food section.

"So what do you do?" He awkwardly asks. You can tell how nervous he is around people.

"I'm a financial analyst in Creave Coeur. But, I'm not sure what's to be analyzed now."

Realizing that life will never be quite the same.

"Yeah, I guess you are right about that."

Victor says, as he stops to think how true Ted's words really are.

"Come on, we better hurry up with this or they might take our food away from us. For tonight atleast."

As, Victor and Ted finish their task on the opposite side of the supermarket, three people are loading lettuce, carrots, and other vegetables stacking them onto a dolly. The three people comprise of: Janis along with two teenage boys. Around the corner the boys push the dolly. One is holding the crates, keeping them from falling off. Janis, approaches the store manager, the two boys are already waiting for her impatiently.

"Hey! Has anyone thought of where we are going to cook all of this stuff?"

The group looks around for an answer.

"Take it over the deli, there's a range there." The Bosnian manager says.

"You heard the man, let's go!" She says as she smacks at the boy pushing the dolly.

The teenager follows her towards the deli located on the far right hand side of the store. Everything is flowing well for the group, as everyone puts their personal differences aside for the collective good of the group.

As, the vegetables and assorted fruit's are delivered behind the counter of the sparsely stocked deli. At the front of the store there is a loud, startling sound of crashing glass moments later, it is combined with the crashing of the aluminum shelf which was loaded with the heavy goods. Everyone inside is startled that the shelf fell, but now the creatures are feverishly trying to get inside and consume the occupants.

Instead of panicking and freaking out. In the process letting the situation spiral out of control. The group accesses the situation in front of them. Addresses, it swiftly before the creatures have a chance to stream inside.

Five men and three woman quickly, run to the shelf and struggle against the army of creatures to lift the shelf back up. The eight people manage to push the creatures back from the supermarket window. Each person pushes against them with all their might. With the extra effort coming from additional people. The shelf goes back up and the creatures are pushed out again. Without interruption, they scramble to fill the shelf space back up. They will need heavier items in order to secure the shelf.

"We're gonna need a lot more stuff here!"

Yells a older black male.

"Victor, bring those carts over here quick!" Ted yells to him.

Running quickly, over to a little cove where the shopping carts are stored. Frantically, he grabs a hold of seven carts pushing with all his might, he gets the carts over to support the shelves. Victor manages to get the carts to Ted in time. As, soon as the carts are there, forty pound sacks of rice are thrown on top of each other. Followed quickly, by several more.

From the far right hand side of the store, between the canned good aisle and the baked goods, a teenager is desperately, trying to keep his grip on the four twelve packs of soda in his hand.

"Go grab the rest of them and bring them over!"

A black male in his twenties says to everyone. It's a novel idea making a wall where there was no wall with literally hundreds of twelve pack cases. The manager yells out.

"Grab some carts and fill them up with the cases!"

Victor and Ted run to the cove and grabs two more carts.

"Let's go!"

Yells, Ted as they attempt to secure more carts to build the barrier. With the shelf back up, more weight is continuing to be added to support it against the onslaught. The shelf is keeping the creatures back, as further reinforcements of supplies come. Suddenly, the creatures begin to back off of their attack. Perhaps they see another way inside or maybe they don't think they can get inside the market and give up. The creatures retreat doesn't install compliancy in the supermarket dwellers, they continue to refortify the shelves along it's entire length. They can't afford another weak spot. If, the creatures found one, there may be others along the line.

Did they successfully manage to turn the creatures away successfully? Or, instead are the creatures waiting to strike with even more vengeance in a time of their choosing? Nobody knows for sure, they'll only know for sure when they attack again. The people inside know they can't rest.

Slam!

The front door vibrates and shakes, as a group of creatures run full speed and slam into the automatic door. Though the doors stay upright and withstood a hard hit, they can't take many more like that.

"Move the registers over to the doors, quickly!"

The two cashiers along with three others roll the registers over to the doors. With the registers in place, it provides greater protection. Again, the creatures run and smack hard against the Plexiglas and steel framed door. The Plexiglas windows are beginning to crack.

"We need something else!"

Ted yells over to the group.

"What?!" She pleads

"Something! Anything that's heavy!" He yells.

"Watch out!"

Is yelled out, as the cash register is turned over by the creatures breaking though the Plexiglas door, pushing the top heavy register over. The inside of the supermarket turns into complete chaos. The uprooted cash register smashes against the remaining two registers. Causing them to scatter to the middle of the store. Ted and Janis are knocked down by the thunderous registers. The registers finally come to stop against the service counter. Then they flip over on their sides.

"We gotta fight them!"

Screams Ted in obvious pain as, he struggles to get back to his feet. Three of the men that were transporting the soda cases come running with shovels from aisle eleven: the accessory aisle. The creatures have just stepped foot inside and already that's farther then the group would like them to be.

WHACK!! A sick, dull sounding thud resonates, as the first man to encounter the ghoul. Delivers a smashing metal shovel hard against the walking dead creature's skull. Though his hit is solid and on the money, the creature continues it's pursuit of the brick layer. He quickly backs up, and swings again. This time, he puts even more power behind the swing. There's a pulsating feeling of hatred toward these damn creatures. Running through the veins of everyone in the store.

This swing is better for the bricklayer, the curved head of the shovel tears into the soft and mushy brain of the creature. The creature's brain is exposed by it's cracked skull. The color inside, is a muted silver grayish color. The creature continues to stagger on spaghetti legs for three more steps. Then the creature takes a header on the right side of it's lifeless body. Only three creatures managed to enter though the opening in the automatic doors. Already one has been killed, so the focus shifts to preventing more from entering. The other members of the group focuses on exterminating the remaining two creatures.

"Help me flip these registers back over!"

Ted says limping with his ankle bleeding from the blow. The manager and two of the cashiers run over and attempt to get the registers up right. The cash register crashes with metal and plastic clanging together, as they turn back up. Ted limps all the way over to the service doors.

"Do you have them?"

The brick layer yells out to the two other men. They don't answer him instead they each go after one creature. The creatures go wild once inside the supermarket. Quickly, they scatter in such an unorganized fashion that it's impossible to predict what direction they'll go next.

"Come here you motha fucka!"

The man says as, he slips falling to the ground. While trying to catch up with the ghoul.

"I need some help!"

The fallen man pleads for back up. The bricklayer hears him and steps up trying to catch up to the creature, which has now made it's way in the store where the check-out registers used to be.

"Watch out!"

He warns the others that lie within the creatures reach. Everyone scatters to get away from a possible bite and the extinction of their humanity.

"Come Here!"

The bricklayer mutters in a low tone to himself. He clenches his teeth together and swings for the back of the ghoul's head.

CLANG!!! The impact forces the creature to fall flat on it's face. The man that fell arrives at the scene. All the sudden, he begins attacking the creature viciously. Blow after blow as, the shovel lands on the creatures battered skull. The shovel inflects so much damage that the skull literally collapses in, on itself. The creature's face becomes bit's of mush. Pieces of brain and skull begin to stick to his shovel.

"Stop!"

The bricklayer shouts to the out of control man. It's not until the bricklayer grabs the man that the shovel hits the creature for the last time.

"Don't lose it man, we still gots tons of shit to deal with."

The bricklayer let's go of his arm. Finally the man backs away from the destroyed creature. He can not bring himself to even look at it, as he turns his head away from the stricken creature.

"Yeah, lets get that last one!"

The man says as they both join the third man, who is finishing off the last of the creatures. Which managed to breach through the automatic door. The creature is knocking over displays at the end of each aisle, as it flees from the man. The creature stumbles as, it rounds a corner tripping over a display of on-sale canned vegetables. At the entrance of aisle eight with the display of Pepsi two liter bottles, the creature falls into the display and they begin to roll across the store in every direction. The awkward moving creature steps on a spinning bottle of Mountain Dew and falls on aisle nines display of potato chips. Frantically, the creature tries to escape from the pile of sour cream, BBQ and salt and vinegar potato chip bags. Finally, the creature manages to get back to it's clumsy feet.

"Now!"

Ted yells for the three men to seize upon this opportunity to finish the final creature.

"I got it!"

The man yells, as he is a mere six feet from the ghoul, just a little out of range to inflict optimal damage on the creature with the shovel. The creature begins to run again when the third man hits the creature from behind. It's not a solid hit because the two were both moving when he swung for the creature. But, it's good enough of a strike to knock the creature down. It also gives the other two men pursuing, the necessary time to catch up and deal with the creature. The man is shocked when the slowing creature freaks out turning 360 degrees back towards him.

"Fucking help me out!"

He yells to get the two other men to help him with this out of control creature.

"I am there!"

The bricklayer says, as he carefully navigates his way over and through the hundreds of soda bottles. As, well as the slickness that it created when the two liter bottles broke open leaking on the industrial vinyl flooring. The floor is very slick, making it very easy to fall and bust your backside. The bricklayer leaves no doubt, as to his intentions. The swing of the shovel makes the air around it, howl as it fly's towards it's target.

BAMM! The shovel connects with the skull and split's it at the brain stem. The side of the shovel penetrates through the skin. Still, the creature continues towards the out of position man. He raises his weapon ready to strike again. From behind, the third man smashes the shovel against the skull of the wobbly ghoul. The creature staggers still closer to the man in front of it. The desire to feed still burns so deep in the genetic make up of the creature, it can't give up.

Not until the brain is totally destroyed. The man in front of the creatures smacks it over it's head for third time. The final blow from the shovel finishes it off, this time the creature dies for good. The creature let's out one last low eerie moan. With the danger apparently over, four men and women finish the blocking off of the automatic doors. The group has overcome this life threatening attack. They turned chaos into teamwork. They faced the challenges together and picked up where one fell.

Others rose when the stricken group member fell. St. Louis is emersed in this outbreak and the entire city is overwhelmed. The inhabitants of this Food World store are on their own. From the outside looking in they have seemed to find a niche for themselves in this chaotic new world. The order of dominance has been reversed from humans, as the dominate species, to the area around St. Louis being at the mercy of some strange and unexplainable horror. Is the city on the brink of extinction? The metropolitan population in excess of 2.4 million is now less than 50,000. Not even four hours after the first outbreak victim. The creatures have asserted their total dominance and reign over their new territory.

26

5:17 P.M. OCTOBER 28, 2006

With I-70 in their sights all which remains is, the odd lone creature walking awkwardly searching along the now abandoned and deserted streets of Downtown St. Louis. WRAMM, the engine of the motorcycle revs before Lance puts the transmission into gear and pulls away from the intersection of 4th Street and Broadway. The exhaust hums, as he slowly approaches the intersection cautiously. He doesn't run through it blindly. He's aware and doesn't want to get caught up in an ambush by those creatures, as they lie in wait. No, discretion is the better part of valor in this situation.

"Are you sure about this?"

Leah leans up to ask him, who is scanning back and forth across the streets looking for anything that can potentially jump out at him.

"Maybe we should just find a safe place to hide."

She says to him. He is still not certain, there is nothing here.

"There is no where to hide, they're every fuckin' place. This is the only way left!"

VROOM! He applies more throttle and the bike takes off. Under the overpass they go up the on ramp to I-70, which is just one hundred and fifty feet away. This on ramp as with most lanes of the highway are hopelessly clogged with cars which were left behind. During the first wave of attack's. Either the people fled before the attacks or were killed. You can't move five feet in any direction without stepping in pools of blood or pieces of disposed flesh. Mixed among the rivers and pools of blood are the body parts of the victims. From slivers of skin to parts of the victims along with pieces of broken and smashed teeth floating at the surface of the pools. If the two were operating anything other than a motorcycle or a tank, they would be sunk. Luckily, the nimble bike can maneuver, with great ease.

Half way up the steep on ramp, Leah becomes too aware of the horror which took place in this area two hours prior. A young child of no more than three is lying against the guardrail. Her light blonde hair is saturated in crimson blood. It's fragile tiny body destroyed by the creatures. Leah's heart sinks and she feels nauseous and uneasy. Suddenly, her head begins to feel disoriented and her extremities begin to feel numb. Under normal circumstances, she would have vomited and fainted for sure, but times have changed.

A person never gets used to seeing murder and destruction of your own kind, but you have to deal with it and some how move-on. You can't stop to dwell on it, you need to accept the situation and move forward. It's that or simply just give up and die. She shakes the horrible feelings inside her and squeezes Lance's sternum even tighter. Carefully, the bike snakes it's way up the remainder of the on ramp and enters on the highway. He knew it would be a mess on the highway, but until he saw it with his own eyes, he could never had appreciated, the scope of the destruction. It's effected, not only people but an entire culture, and way of life for close to three million people have been destroyed. It's devastation, as far as the eye can see. Wrecked vehicles, fires smolder from the vehicles as they continue to billow out thick black smoke as they burn away.

"We can't make it through, there's just no way!"

Leah says to Lance as they both look at what's ahead of them.

"Yes, we can and we will. We gotta try and get out of this damn city. There's no goddamn way we can hope to survive with all these fuckin' creatures lurking about!"

He has no intention of turning around and getting off the highway. In his mind there is no other escape routes out of St. Louis than this. It's this way or there is no hope for either one of them. The Ducati hums impatiently, as he pilots the bike through a pool of fresh blood. As, the rear tire emerges from the pool it spit's up blood as the tire struggles to find the necessary grip. At last, the bike finds traction and jumps away from the obstacle. The tread from the bike's tire leaves an imprint in the sticky goo.

Up, ahead on the highway, three quarters of a mile northwest on I-70. Lance can see movement. He spots a group of about twenty people. Walking calmly north to a seemingly common destination. At this distance it is impossible for him to tell if they're human or creature.

"You see that up ahead?"

Lance leans back to ask Leah if she can but to also reassure himself that he is actually seeing people or whatever they might be.

"What are you going to do?"

She asks Lance who is in his own mind and doesn't hear anything she's said. Instead, he runs through the scenarios himself.

"What if their creatures up a head? If it's those damn things, I can just turn around and easily out run them. If they're cool then they might be able to help, if not fuck 'em, we'll leave their asses behind."

"All right, we're going to check this out and see if their cool. They might be able to really help us get out of here."

He knows just what and how to say 'it', to Leah reassuring her. More importantly, for him, to get her to do as he wants. From a near stop the engine revs to life again.

WHAM! WHAM! The powerful engine cranks the horsepower out and a growl from the exhaust exits along with a thick cloud of carbon monoxide.

In between a sea of abandoned vehicles of every make, model and year possible. Lance weaves the motorcycle in and out of their confines with relatively no trouble. Swinging the bike at low speeds, he finally passes Biddle Street, which is only a half mile from where they entered on I-70 at the 3rd Street entrance ramp.

Moving closer to the scene, has not helped Lance in his quest to identify if the people up ahead are good or not.

All he can see is their backs so far, the group up ahead either doesn't hear the loud motorcycle or they don't care about the sounds behind them. Regardless, he continues to maneuver through the mess. Past Biddle, I-70 begins to bend towards the west. It's at this point where the group in front of them stops. The members begin opening the doors to the vehicles. They are pulling people out of the cars to the highway. But, why? Are they injured and need assistance or are is something else going on, all together?

"Damn! I just can't tell what's going on up there?"

Lance yells inside of himself and even shows his outward frustrations by slamming his fist down on the handle grip. Still, after having serious reservations, he continues to take Leah and himself into a situation, that he doesn't feel 100% certain about.

On the narrow vibrating rear seat behind him, Leah worries about what might be up ahead on I-70. In her head all she thinks of all, is the horrible images which she has witnessed today. Then her thoughts move to what happened to her friends throughout the city. To all of those people she loved so much and all the wonderful times she had with them. Now, it's likely they're either dead or one of those creatures. Everyone, she loves in this world has been ripped from her.

They all told her that she had to get away from Lance and his mental abuse. After every beating, he would make it seem, as if it was her fault. Now, when he hit's her, in some way, something she did or said forced him to. She believes it is her fault. Now, with everyone gone forever all she has left in this world is Lance. Funny how things turn out, huh?

Closer now, Lance can begin to make out the people that are being pulled from their autos. They're bloody and motionless, as they lie on the roadway. But, he still can't figure out what the group is up to. They're not treating or helping the injured, nor are they attacking the defenseless potential victims. They are just kind of removing the people and collecting the occupants outside of their respective vehicles. Even at a thousand feet away, the group ahead pays no attention to the motorcycle.

Finally, as he comes to a complete stop with the bike turned at an angle. This is where if forced, he can easily turn around, heading back towards the south. He turns the bike's ignition off and disembarks from the bike, as does Leah. He carefully walks around the wrecked rear end of a Chevy Tahoe that is entangled with a bright red tiny sports car. The diminutive car's front end is wrapped around the rear steel bumper of the hulking suv. He quietly maneuvers over the front end of the car and is now on the shoulder of I-70 looking directly at the group further north.

As, one of the members of the group, a tall husky man wearing a straw cowboy hat turns around to arrange a body from the van that is laying on it's side. Both Lance and Leah get a perfect view of this particular member of the group. The astonishment on both of their faces tells the story of the ghastly images which both of them are experiencing. The person carrying the occupant is a creatures! It's face is torn up from a infectious bite by one of it's fellow creatures.

Dried blood is caked on it's cheek as, well as down the creatures neck. The blue denim buttoned up shirt it's wearing has turned purple from the blood which ran after the attack. But, even with this amount of damage done, it doesn't appear to hinder the creatures. The bodies below on the highway, are either gargling in pain or lying motionless as more people are continued to be pulled out and pilled on top of each other.

Approximately, forty people have been pilled up, their strange and odd behavior being's now to make sense. All twenty members of the group stop as if given a command from a leader, yet not a word was spoken. In unison they converge on the helpless men and women lying unable to escape or defend themselves. It is a perfect slaughter for the creatures. Their food is just sitting there waiting for them to strike. Body after body is torn, as the creatures take their share from each and every unfortunate person lying on the highway.

For the creatures this was an extremely effective way to swell their ranks by more and strategically it, decreased their opponents numbers. Lance and Leah are filled with disgust and disbelief. They struggle to comprehend what their witnessing. Still, the group of creatures don't appear to see them. The likely hood of being seen and attacked by the creatures is very, very high. But, their safe for the moment. They'd find little comfort in this, since they've been forced to view and live through these events.

"We're going to have to turn back, we won't make it past them."

He whispers to Leah.

Turning around to see exactly, what's going on behind them. He wants to be sure things haven't changed. It looks promising and he can't see any obvious signs of creatures lurking about. Leah thinks to herself, how stupid it was to come this way and that she even told this. She knows there's no point in mentioning it. Then, for the first time a thought pops in her head.

"If I get the chance, I'll leave his ass behind! He doesn't know what he's doing anyway. I mean look, we should've got out of here when this first started, but because of him we didn't. Now look at where we are."

"I am going to push the bike fifty feet out, start it and get out of here, ok?"

Lance asks, but he already plans on doing it his way. He crouches, as low as possible and still be able to push the motorcycle in between the many obstacles of cars and trucks. Silently, he manages to get the motorcycle to roll. Thankfully, this stretch of I-70 has a slight downward slope. A gust of cooler air blows east from the Illinois side of the river. The gusts are strong over the Mississippi River. The air blows against the left side of his motorcycle causing the Ducati to wiggle. He gains control over the bike while Leah is close behind him.

When, Lance feels he's far enough away, without warning he jumps on the bike. A twist of the key and the 800 cc engine revs to life. Leah scrambles to hop on the back of the bike before he leaves her behind.

"Hurry up!"

Lance yells at her, seemingly not to care if she's prepared. If, he had told her what he was planning, she could have been prepared.

She's on, but just barely. He gases the throttle and the bike loudly moves away. The group of creatures, are startled by the sudden loud noise. They desire to attack, but know the humans are too far away. Still, the creatures put an effort chasing after the fleeing humans. Lance takes a look over his shoulder, to see them trying in vain to chase after them. Witnessing this, he cracks a smile getting a laugh out of it. He laughs at how stupid these creatures seem to be for chasing after him, even though there's no chance for them to ever to catch up.

More so, Lance is annoyed that his escape plan was thwarted by the large group blocking any hope of escaping via I-70.

"So what now?"

Lance ponders Leah's idea of hiding in a safe building and just hoping that an army of these things doesn't breakdown the door.

"They'll eat us alive. Like they've done to almost everyone in St. Louis. No, that dumb bitch can't be right. Can she?" Thinks Lance to himself.

He dismisses the idea completely. The only reason because Leah came up with it and not him. What a piece of work he truly is.

"We're getting off and following Broadway, south. It's' too crowded, we can't get through there."

She leans forward to hear the new plan he has conjured up.

"Great."

Is all she can say as, he maneuvers the opposite direction down the entrance ramp to I-70. Without sight he, passes the body of that child, who was slaughtered, so viciously. This time though she looks away from the horrible sight while he is busy scanning the roadway below. It finally looks clear. Lance powers the bike around the left side of an eighteen-wheeler that has a trailer full of hogs. The frightened animals have been rooting and snorting in a desperate attempt to escape from their metal prison.

Back on 4th Street, Lance has a clear path that is free of smashed and wrecked autos. Quickly, he goes through the gears. He's in third gear by this time and traveling sixty miles an hour. The road is badly torn up in this area, so Leah holds on for dear life as, he maneuvers the bike down the treacherous road. Bump after bump is soaked up by the cycle's suspension and she is jarred by each one. She withstands all the jerks and turbulence thrown at her. Quickly, Lance hangs a left onto Broadway and takes the turn with too much speed. He goes to wide on the entrance and ends up inches form smashing the bike into the curb.

At the speed their traveling it would've surely severely injured or killed them. But, luck is with him once again, as he manages to wrangle the bike to stick on the road. He's been lucky so far and with this much luck, he should have played the slots in Vegas before this plague hit the city. He's put that white-knuckle moment behind him and continues south on Broadway.

The streets here are not as densely filled with the abandoned vehicles, but the signs of the outbreak surround them. There are more mangled and twisted remains of those who have succumbed to the creatures, as they advanced through the city. High above the road, in the high rise building's above. Bodies dangle outside the broken and smashed windows. The bodies are those, who attempted to jump to their death rather then suffer a grueling death. Within inches from a death they had chosen for themselves, they were captured and forced to suffer at the hands of creatures in the last moments of their life. Down below the broken windows, blood drips on the sidewalk.

Flies, gnats, and other insects buzz the bodies and excrement's expelled from the corpses. The smell of death is overwhelming. Thankfully, Lance is moving fast enough that the air which passes by him then around Leah's nose is faint enough to keep the stench from gagging her. Block after block; Locust, Olive, Pine, tens of thousands of people are just plain missing presumed to be dead.

In five hours the creatures destroyed an area that more than forty years of urban sprawl and white flight could not. She sees the devastation, but has grown immune to it's effects. The intersection at Chestnut is littered with a spectacular crash. A school bus was apparently driving east on Chestnut and a full size Chevy pickup truck, ran the light at Broadway in a panicked attempt to flee. The smashed bus was subsequently smashed from behind, the aftermath a multi car pile up. There are no creatures lurking about except for the occasional loner, clumsy walking around.

It seems to observe them, that the creatures are hyper aggressive when they're packed densely into groups. Yet, when alone, they present little or no challenge. Inside a group of more than five. They transform into a vicious nightmare. Lance elects to hop the curb avoiding the melee of the wreck. Slowly, the back tire of the bike clears the curb. When it connects with the sidewalk the bike growls as it finally motors away. He now proceeds at a crawl. The bikes exhaust noise is bouncing Waw! Waw! The noise resonates in between the brick buildings of Chestnut.

The loud cracking noise doesn't help avoiding the unwanted attention of the creatures. He knows this and tries his best to get through the intersection as quickly as possible. But, it's so messed up with tempered shards of broken automobile glass covering the area.

"God, I hope I don't pop at tire."

Lance says to God himself. Finally, sticking the front end of the Ducati in the clear, he finally puts Chestnut behind him. He then begins to think about how clear everything is right now. He's not thinking that a surprise could be around the corner. It's his cockiness and short sightless that makes, so many people dislike him. Not like, he gives a shit less if they do or not. The periodic rains that have been brewing all day long begin again. It's a light drizzle barely covering the ground. The tiny drops mixed with the cool fall breeze, brings a chill to their bones.

It's growing dark now at 5:30 PM, Leah on the back of the motorcycle shivers as the cool air rips right through her body. She can't stop chattering her teeth.

"I want off this bike, now!"

She thinks to herself as the bike vibrates and jars away at her body so roughly. Lance approaches Market Street, the traffic lights, as well as the streetlights aren't working. This entire area is dark and quiet except for the drops of the rain hitting the road. He begins thinking, what it is he's trying to achieve. In the middle of the street, he pauses the Ducati in the middle of the intersection.

The old courthouse lies to his left. On the grounds are a group of five creatures that roam the marbled steps of the former hall of justice.

They hear the now rare sound of people. Before they actually have sight of the humans, the creatures were complacent merely stumbling around. When they see not one but two humans. The five creatures are whipped in a feeding frenzy. Without warning the creatures charge towards Lance and Leah in a rapid strike. So fast, that Lance is caught by surprise. Because he doubted that the creatures could charge that fast. They are now two hundred feet away and closing fast on the two.

There's still plenty of time for them to escape before the creatures get to them, but he doesn't have a clue where he wants to go or what he wants to do. Does, he want to continue down Market? Get off and try to find a safe spot in a building? For the first time since this outbreak started, he doesn't have a clue, as to what he should do. He is consumed with doubt, causing him to panic. He stands hovering with the bike at a stop, it is still idling at the intersection. Meanwhile, Leah sees just how close the creatures are getting to them. She takes a bold step of hitting Lance in the back to snap him out of it of his haze.

Finally, he goes hastily continuing ahead on Market. Leaving the excited and disappointed creatures behind empty handed. He swings his head back and forth looking for any possible place that's safe enough to stop and regain his bearings. He finds a good spot past the old Busch Stadium on Poplar Street in an empty parking lot. The lot was used for parking at the Cardinal baseball games. This is a good one, because it's an open area. Allowing him to spot any creatures that might find them an inviting target.

"Do you want to find some place and hide? We can block the door up and make it super strong!"

Lance is talking so fast.

"You made us come out of our apartment pass up tons of chances and now you want to find a place to hide?"

She says, as obviously she is angered and totally frustrated in his total screwing up of the situation.

"Look, I thought we could get through the mess on that motorcycle but there's just no where to run. There's no Emerald City at the end of Market, there's nothing but more of those things!"

This is his closest he's come to admitting that, he royally messed everything up.

"Where should we look?"

He asks her, like she will say.

"Sure, we're on Market and Poplar so the best hiding place would be…"

"We need to find a secure basement. That way there's only one way in so those things won't be able to get us!"

Lance says, as he discovers his epiphany

"That's it! That's what we're going to do? We came all this way and all that we had to do, was just walk down to the basement at our apartment?"

She says, as she begins to boil with anger. A risky move for her, considering his track record.

"Look, I tried…"

Is the only thing he says as he walks away towards Market.

"We can't get back to the apartment, it's too thick around Washington Avenue. We have to find one close around here somewhere."

Lance, says as his eyes begin to scout for a possible location. As he walks around the loose gravel stone lot, his shoes crunch the slogged wet gravel. He notices a pub restaurant, just forty feet away.

He runs over to the establishment and notices something very important. In the sidewalk there are two metal doors that if opened. Lead, down to a storage/prep area of this restaurant. The location appears safe. The people which might of been there now are gone. The only evidence of the outbreak in this restaurant lies on the wood floors. There's blood along the floor then smeared along the bar. The same blood which coats most of the city now. Convinced that the location is safe, Lance hurries back to Leah. She's standing not five feet from the motorcycle. She's obviously nervous, she's darting her eyes back and forth looking. Searching for anything which might be out of the ordinary. But, in today's world that isn't hard."

"I found the perfect place!"

Lance shouts to her from over twenty five feet away. She looks around in a dejected way. Her eyes are glazed over and don't appear to see what is happening. All she wants is for this to be over with. Tired of what is happening around. She's exhausted and wants to escape from this. She wants things to be the way they were. The despair has began to set in for her.

"Come on lets' go."

Says, Lance. She doesn't respond. The light rain continues to fall. Her light brown leather jacket is soaked by the on again, off again rain.

"Hey, lets go, this place is perfect."

He says again trying to coax her into hurrying up. Then getting her down in the, storage area. Finally, away from any possible danger. He is now standing next to her.

"Hey, what's your deal? Let's go!"

Again he talks to her, but she still doesn't respond to him. But, instead she follows him, as he returns towards the restaurant. The light rain has changed, again this to a downpour. The big hard drops of rain beat upon their heads and shoulders. The stings make Lance grimace, all he really wants is to get out of the open and into the dry and safeness of the basement. Leah on the other hand, feels the opposite. The cold rain provides her with the much needed wake up call. It's so refreshing to feel something other than the numbness that's been inside of her all day long.

"How bad is this place?"

She asks, Lance who is thinking of nothing but getting inside. He doesn't bother to answer her questions.

Finally, they both make it to the safety and protection of the restaurant and out of the pouring rain. The building is quite and still. The only two sounds that are audible are the sounds of the rain hitting the aluminum awning. The second is the squawking of a flock of crows flying south.

"Well let's get in and see what it looks like."

He says to her, as she shakes off the rain that has her soaked her to the bone. Lance shuts and secures the wooden door that has a shinny brass style door handle. He looks the place over, his eyes glance over the splattered blood, which is everywhere. He knows that every place in the city has been a scene of at least one attack today. Leah also takes the sights with a cool attitude toward what she observes.

All she wants to do is get down in that basement. Forgetting that today October 28, 2006 ever happened.

"We even got a lot of food. Enough to last us for week's maybe even a month."

Lance declares as he explores the kitchen area. Food's the last thing on her mind. A nice pair of dry clothes would be ideal. The interior of the restaurant is growing dark, it's hard to distinguish where the booths and benches are.

"They have candles on the tables." Says Leah who notices each table has a candle and a vase.

"I'll find some matches. They gotta have 'em back here."

Says Lance as he goes off to the customers area where the tables are. Then into the employee area where the wait staff preps the food. Through the dim lighting conditions, he finds a box of matches. Which will enable him to achieve enough light, so they won't smash their knees and shins against the unforgiving wooden booths. He lights the candles at each of the eight tables. Now that they have some light, Leah checks the dead bolt. As, well as the sliding bolt at the bottom of the door. The candlelight flickers as the fire burns the wick further and further with each passing moment.

"Hey, I am hungry. Let's find something to eat."

Mentions Lance. She walks towards the kitchen with caution. Today has taught her to take nothing for granted. Lance doesn't find much food. upstairs It appears the restaurant used the upstairs, as a kitchen. Using the basement as the food storage area.

"Leah grab a candle for me, I want to go down stairs. I can't see shit."

He says, as she walks over to a long eight person table and removes two candleholders. Lance grabs a hold of the candleholder and begins to walk down the greasy, slippery wooden steps. There is a landing which splits the staircase in the middle. The steps are so greasy and slick from the dirty dishes that are carried down to be washed. Additionally, the steps are permanently soiled by dirt and grime which does not clean up from the daily borage that a restaurant is exposed to.

Possibly, if there was more light, Lance would be able to see the blood that has overpowered the salt, which was thrown down in attempts to neutralize the grease. The steps along with the stonewall are covered as the blood drips. The humidity downstairs hasn't allowed the liquids to completely dry and evaporate. The basement has an odd smell. It is not a bad smell, but not a just a typical restaurant scent. Lance rationalizes the odor, must have trickled down from the carnage upstairs. Leah stands on the landing, between the basement and the upstairs. She's frightened and doesn't know what to do next. It's funny how a basement can be a scary place to be, even under normal circumstances. Add the outbreak of the living dead and the emotions you feel escalate one hundred times. The dishwashing machine is straight ahead from Lance. The walk in freezer to his right and beyond that is a storage area. To the left of the dishwasher is a doorway which leads into an area used for a storage and a small office.

Lance walks towards the food storage to see what's there. Meanwhile, inside the room a medal rack stocked with bottles of cleaning supplies and garbage bags crashes to the floor. The thunderous noise startles both of them with Leah jumping like a jackrabbit up five of the stairs. Lance knows, he has to find out what the source of the noise. He turns his attention away from the rummaging for food. A second door is on his far right and leads to the storage area. Lance believes his best bet is to flank around the source of the sound. The storage room is completely dark and he can't see without the aid of his candlelight.

It's pitch black in the basement. There's not even a hint of outside light because there are no windows. The luxury of electricity is long gone. He walks through the room slowly and cautiously, being sure to take in each and every item in the room, he encounters. A slop sink to fill up the mop buckets is along the wall as, well as paint cans and brushes stored along a pillar in the center of the room. Finding nothing so far, Lance is now waiting for something to pop out at him. He walks further, saying to himself.

"There's nothing back here, the shelf just must have fell over."

"Leah, it's' cool, there's nothing down here."

Yells Lance to Leah. She's at the top of the stairs and as far away as possible from the downstairs steps.

"Are you sure?" She inquires

"Come on!"

Responds Lance, "Chicken shit" is mumbled under his breathe. She cautiously comes down the last step and is now standing on the little cove where they keep the masses of plates, bowls and other dishware.

"Lance?" She says, wondering where in the dark, he is.

"Yeah." He says, as he walks up just feet from her. She is startled and jumps.

"Shit! Don't do that again!" She yells.

They both walk over to the pantry, he is eager to demonstrate his gathering abilities.

"Damn, look at all this food we got! We got it all!" Lance exclaims.

WHACK! Upstairs the door which leads from the kitchen to the outside is slammed shut, extremely hard.

"What the hell was that?"

She needs to hear the sound upstairs is nothing to worry about. Lance, doesn't take the time to answer her. Instead, he runs up the steps taking three of the slick steps at a time. The once quite upstairs has been transformed into a thunderous barrage of stomps and wails.

"God damn it!"

Yells, Lance at the top of the steps. Then he jumps for the landing and hurries back down the remaining four steps.

"Come on, we gotta hide!"

He screams to her, as he frantically searches for a safe place. But, he can not find a good place. Everything here has either a simple wooden door or no door at all. Nothing is solid enough. These doors may hold off one creatures for a while, but they'll continue to pile up. And, as more and more do, the crazed creatures will get through anything.

"We can't use any of this; we need to get in the freezer."

Lance says. Knowing the implications of what he said.

"No way! We can't we do that! We have to do something else, we'll die in there."

Leah says frantically, as she tries to think of an alternative. Nothing is coming to her.

"There's not!"

She can feel the urgency in his voice. Right then she knows, there is no other options which will work for them.

"Fine."

Is all she can mutter, as Lance opens the latch to the walk in cooler. If he had a clear mind and enough time, he would have noticed the temperature inside of the walk in freezer reads thirty five degrees, just a mere three degrees above freezing.

A human can survive less than twenty minutes in those extreme conditions without the necessary protection. Even though neither of them have ever stepped foot in this particular restaurant before. Quickly, the two take a final look around. This place now seems so beautiful and important. They know that no matter what, they are never going to come out of this cooler alive. Their are only two options available to them. Are; freeze to death in minutes inside this freezer or succumb to the creatures outside. There is a third possibility, that the creatures will tear the metal door down and overwhelm them.

Their fate is known by only Lance and Leah and possibly the creatures know what is destined for them. But, this applies to a large extent to St. Louis, as well. After six hours since the first case on Highway 44, the population of three million has been slaughtered, reduced to less than six thousand now. From within the cooler, comes one voice followed moments later by a second and final voice. Afterwards, silence falls over the city.

"I'm cold, Lance."
"I'm sorry for everything……."

Epilogue

31 October 2006
From: The Department of Defense
To: The President of the United States

Subject: Assessment of destruction, St. Louis, Missouri

The infectious outbreak which has crippled and destroyed St. Louis and the surrounding areas, is containing to spread at explosive rates. I'm sure you are well aware, the city of Chicago is beginning to receive an influx of the infected dead.

This Department recommends a quarantine of the entire midwestern section of The United States. The area needs to be sealed off, as soon as possible to to contain the infection. The technicians within this department have accomplished, an extensive analysis of the available data.

The results from the simulation are catastrophic. Up to this point, 8.5 million civilians have been contaminated. Fear and panic over the outbreak has caused the economy to collapse over 30 percent. All of our, Allies have placed an embargo on our outbound vessels. Due to the overwhelming panic amongst the civilian population, Martial Law has been imposed.

You must react now. The consequences of your inaction will be fatal to this country. This Department recommends to you, that we first use our air power to initially eliminate some of their overwhelming numbers. Then the second phase, is to call in our Special Forces Units to terminate them and abolish the virus. Sir, we cannot afford to procrastinate on this. The time to react is now. We must destroy, these creatures before they destroy us.

THE END

978-0-595-35934-9
0-595-35934-5

Printed in the United Kingdom
by Lightning Source UK Ltd.
114379UKS00001B/253